Slocum half turned, but something hard and heavy crashed into the side of his head, knocking him to the ground. Stunned, he lay there. Through pain-misted eyes, he saw a boot kicking straight for his belly. He curled up in a tight ball and brought his arms around in time to rob the blow of much of its power.

Slocum forced himself outward, got his hands and knees under him, then pushed to his feet. He swung around and caught a hard fist to the belly that almost knocked the wind from him. Doubling over, he grabbed and caught a second fist coming to add to the damage of the first. He clung to the arm with all his strength, then spun enough to drive his shoulder into his attacker's chest, knocking him back.

Slocum let go and stumbled back. He grabbed for his six-shooter and drew.

He had Randall Bray dead in his sights.

"Don't go for it. You'll be dead before you clear leather," Slocum warned.

Bray ignored him and grabbed for the pistol at his hip . . .

DON'T MISS THESE ALL-ACTION WESTERN SERIES FROM THE BERKLEY PUBLISHING GROUP

THE GUNSMITH by J. R. Roberts

Clint Adams was a legend among lawmen, outlaws, and ladies. They called him . . . the Gunsmith.

LONGARM by Tabor Evans

The popular long-running series about Deputy U.S. Marshal Custis Long—his life, his loves, his fight for justice.

SLOCUM by Jake Logan

Today's longest-running action Western. John Slocum rides a deadly trail of hot blood and cold steel.

BUSHWHACKERS by B. J. Lanagan

An action-packed series by the creators of Longarm! The rousing adventures of the most brutal gang of cutthroats ever assembled—Quantrill's Raiders.

DIAMONDBACK by Guy Brewer

Dex Yancey is Diamondback, a Southern gentleman turned con man when his brother cheats him out of the family fortune. Ladies love him. Gamblers hate him. But nobody pulls one over on Dex . . .

WILDGUN by Jack Hanson

The blazing adventures of mountain man Will Barlow—from the creators of Longarm!

TEXAS TRACKER by Tom Calhoun

J.T. Law: the most relentless—and dangerous—manhunter in all Texas. Where sheriffs and posses fail, he's the best man to bring in the most vicious outlaws—for a price.

JAKE LOGAN

SLOCUM AND THE DIRTY DOZEN

J

JOVE BOOKS, NEW YORK

THE BERKLEY PUBLISHING GROUP
Published by the Penguin Group
Penguin Group (USA) Inc.
375 Hudson Street, New York, New York 10014, USA
Penguin Group (Canada), 90 Eglinton Avenue East, Suite 700, Toronto, Ontario M4P 2Y3, Canada
(a division of Pearson Penguin Canada Inc.)
Penguin Books Ltd., 80 Strand, London WC2R 0RL, England
Penguin Group Ireland, 25 St. Stephen's Green, Dublin 2, Ireland (a division of Penguin Books Ltd.)
Penguin Group (Australia), 250 Camberwell Road, Camberwell, Victoria 3124, Australia
(a division of Pearson Australia Group Pty. Ltd.)
Penguin Books India Pvt. Ltd., 11 Community Centre, Panchsheel Park, New Delhi—110 017, India
Penguin Group (NZ), 67 Apollo Drive, Rosedale, North Shore 0632, New Zealand
(a division of Pearson New Zealand Ltd.)
Penguin Books (South Africa) (Pty.) Ltd., 24 Sturdee Avenue, Rosebank, Johannesburg 2196,
South Africa

Penguin Books Ltd., Registered Offices: 80 Strand, London WC2R 0RL, England

SLOCUM AND THE DIRTY DOZEN

A Jove Book / published by arrangement with the author

PRINTING HISTORY
Jove edition / October 2010

Cover illustration by Sergio Giovine.

ISBN: 978-0-515-14848-0

JOVE®
Jove Books are published by The Berkley Publishing Group,
a division of Penguin Group (USA) Inc.
375 Hudson Street, New York, New York 10014.
JOVE® is a registered trademark of Penguin Group (USA) Inc.
The "J" design is a trademark of Penguin Group (USA) Inc.

PRINTED IN THE UNITED STATES OF AMERICA

10 9 8 7 6 5 4 3 2 1

1

John Slocum turned a little in the hard chair so his hand would rest closer to the ebony handle of the Colt Navy slung in the cross-draw holster. He had been gambling in the Cross Timbers Saloon for almost twelve hours and never saw a hand like this. He wasn't going to be cheated out of it—and the dealer across from him had been palming cards and adding some from under the table whenever the mood suited him. Slocum hadn't cared since he was never on the losing end of the cheating.

And he wasn't going to start now that he had a real hand.

Ignoring the din around him became easier as he concentrated on the game. Two of the players didn't count. One was a drunk cowboy about ready to topple from his chair and onto the sawdust-covered barroom floor. The other looked to be a lawyer or maybe even the town's doctor. Whatever he was, he played with an intensity that was sure to put even more money into Slocum's pocket.

"I got to raise," the lawyer said, pushing twenty dollars in greenbacks into the pot. The drunk cowboy belched and shoved the rest of his poke in. A quick glance assured Slocum this didn't amount to more than a few dollars.

The real money would come from the gambler to his left.

Slocum didn't have to look at his cards again. The four jacks were burned into his brain. Playing for months on end, he had not seen this good a hand. He almost laughed when the gambler not only matched what both Slocum and the lawyer had put in but upped it another twenty dollars.

It was time to do some acting for an audience of only two since the cowboy had passed out.

"You reckon he wants a card?" the gambler said, looking at the unconscious cowboy as he riffled through the deck of cards in his left hand. "He sure as hell can't stand!"

The man liked his own joke and laughed heartily. Slocum watched what he did with the deck to be sure seconds weren't dealt or some other sleight-of-hand trick did him out of his win.

"Let him be," the lawyer said. "I'm bumping the pot a hundred for him. That's what it'd take to call, right?"

This surprised Slocum and made him wonder if he wasn't being worked from two directions. The gambler might draw his attention while his partner—was he really a lawyer at all?—came in for the kill. This made Slocum warier than ever, watching how the gambler handled the deck and where all the cards went.

All of them, especially those going to the lawyer, who out of some hidden charitable urge kept the cowboy in the game.

"Why you betting his hand as well as your own?" Slocum asked. He worried about the real answer, not the one the lawyer was likely to give. If they had stacked the deck so the lawyer got cards after a certain number were dealt, he had to keep the cowboy in the game. Otherwise, the careful deck stacking would turn his hand to dross when he drew.

"I owe him. He did me a favor a while back. Who knows? He might have the winning hand."

"Are you taking any cards?" the gambler asked. The lawyer took three and waited to see what Slocum did.

There was no call to throw away anything. He couldn't improve on four jacks. Slocum slipped the cards back and forth across the table, then said, "Give me one."

He wanted to see if either the gambler or the lawyer reacted. Neither did, to his surprise. From their reactions, they thought he was drawing to a straight or maybe a flush. But he was definitely on a draw. He read that in their expressions.

The gambler flipped the requested card across the table. Slocum didn't bother looking at it. He bet everything he had, almost a hundred dollars. When he won, he'd have close to five hundred and could get the hell out of Wyoming. The only reason he knew the name of this town—Clabber Crossing—was from the fancy sign erected on the only road in. Whoever Clabber was, he had an inflated sense of his own worth and the town he had no doubt named after himself. He probably considered erecting the fancy sign with its gold lettering and fine carving a civic duty.

"That's a righteous bet, partner," the gambler said. "I have to fold." He tossed his cards to the table.

"What about him?" Slocum asked, pointing to the passed-out cowboy.

"He can't call. He's plumb out of money, and I don't see any point in staking him anymore," the lawyer said. He reached over and pushed the man's cards to the center, where they mingled with the gambler's mucked hand. "But I, on the other hand, have a good hand and I'll raise you five hundred."

"I can't match that," Slocum said. He took a deep breath. "Let me see the color of your money."

"That's not a problem," the lawyer said, adding a thick wad of greenbacks to the pot. He stared hard at Slocum. "You can't call, the pot's mine. Those are the rules."

"I'll call. My horse and gear ought to cover the raise."

"Not even tossing in that well-used six-shooter of yours would match my raise," the lawyer said, "but settle down now." He held up his hand to keep Slocum from drawing his Colt Navy. "You think you got the best hand, don't you?"

That was obvious. Slocum studied the man like a hungry coyote might look at a slow rabbit.

"Now, I have a good hand myself, but I don't gamble for the money. I got all the money there is around here."

"Why do you play cards?" Slocum asked, but he knew the answer.

"I like to win. There's no thrill for me if I pulled in this huge pot because you couldn't match my bet, but there would be if you called and I beat you fair and square. You see, that'd mean I outplayed you. That'd mean I *won*."

"So you'll accept my horse and gear?"

"Not at all. I've got all the horses I want and, no offense, I suspect your gear isn't of the finest quality."

"It's well used," Slocum said. He had been in the saddle too long. Drifting up from New Mexico, he had spent a couple weeks in Denver before getting restless. Word of ranchers needing hands had lured him to this corner of Wyoming, but the rumors had been false. There wasn't a ranch in the area hiring, even a man of Slocum's experience. He had gambled enough to make it worthwhile to stay until now. When he won this pot, he'd be set for months. San Francisco and the fancy clubs on Russian Hill beckoned. He wouldn't have to settle for the dives along the Embarcadero. With those highfalutin clubs came elegant women, and Slocum had been developing a taste for them over the past few months.

If a man didn't sample the best now and again, what was the use of living?

He certainly wasn't going to find it in Clabber Crossing, Wyoming.

"I will accept a different coin," the lawyer said. He glanced down at the six-gun holstered at Slocum's left hip.

"I'm not a gunman, and I don't kill for money."

"Ah, but you have killed. Perhaps when you thought they needed killing."

"I was in the war."

"Of course you were. We all were," the lawyer said, his tone turning grim. The moment passed and he smiled insincerely. "I want service for one month. While you might be required to use your pistol, that is not the primary job. You see, the rodeo is coming to town and that always brings a rowdy element intent on disturbing the peace."

"You're not the town marshal. I don't see a badge pinned to your vest." What Slocum did see was a shoulder rig and a small pistol tucked under the man's left arm.

"You noticed the town's name when you rode into town?"

"Hard to miss," Slocum allowed. "I'd say Clabber is a . . ." He caught himself from saying more since he realized then who his opponent was.

"Yes, many men call me that. I'm Clyde Clabber and this is my town."

"And 'bout everything in it," piped up the gambler. "The Cross Timbers is his and—"

"I made a fortune in lumbering in the Pacific Northwest before coming to Wyoming."

"Where he's made another fortune in cattle raising," the gambler went on as if he hadn't been interrupted. "Fact is, there's not much around here Mr. Clabber doesn't own."

"Except me," Slocum said. "No man owns me."

"I only want to, shall we say, rent your services."

"If you win."

"When I win," Clabber said. His face went expressionless. "Deal? Your expertise for one month?"

Four jacks lay under Slocum's hand. Four. Almost a thousand dollars was in the pot.

"Deal. I call." Slocum turned over the cards. He had

been dealt a deuce as his fifth card, not that it mattered. Nothing was going to beat four jacks.

Clyde Clabber dropped his hand onto the table. Slocum felt as if he had fallen off the highest peak in the Grand Tetons as he stared at four queens.

"Go on, drink up," Clabber offered, pushing the whiskey bottle over to Slocum. After seeing the queens, Slocum had considered backing out of the deal. Clabber would have a sizable pot to content himself, but as he said, it wasn't about the money. Winning mattered the most. "I'm not charging you, Slocum. In fact, I'll probably pay you in ways you never thought you'd see in a town like this."

A sample sip convinced Slocum that the man who owned the town and everything in it had decent taste in whiskey. He did more than wet his lips with the second taste.

"What do you want me to do?" He looked around the saloon and saw some rowdy cowboys pushing and shoving. It wouldn't take much for this roughhousing to end up as a full-fledged brawl. "Break up the fight?"

"Them? No, not at all. I let the fights go on. Keeps the patrons coming back since they've come here to let off steam. What do I care if they bust up the place so long as they pay for it—or their boss does?"

"You got a lock on every door around here. What do you really want from me? It's not the favor of a drinking companion."

Clabber laughed.

"You have quite a sense of humor, Slocum. You're going to fit in just fine. Bring the bottle if you like. Otherwise, let's head out to the edge of town. That's where you're going to work off your month of service."

"Service or servitude?"

"You're a proud man, Slocum. I see that. I have a sense of honor myself, which is why I have need of your services." Clabber walked to the rear of the saloon and left through a door hardly large enough to squeeze through. Slocum followed, having to turn sideways to keep his shoulders from brushing the frame. Clabber was already a ways down the alley behind the saloon. Slocum tried to make out what the other buildings were on the adjoining street, then found himself almost running to catch up. He'd have plenty of time to explore Clabber Crossing if he was stuck here working for Clyde Clabber for a full month.

"There it is," Clabber said. He stopped and stared at a two-story house some distance from the edge of town. "Victorian bric-a-brac, straight from London. Damned expensive, but worth it to keep Severigne happy. You'll like her. I predict you'll want to keep her happy, too."

They went up the steps. To Slocum's surprise, Clabber knocked on the door. For some reason, he'd thought the man would push on inside. The lace curtain hiding the house's interior pulled back, but Slocum couldn't see who peered out. Clabber waited patiently as the door was unlocked and opened to admit him.

"My dear," he said. Slocum thought Clabber might have bent to kiss the woman but couldn't be sure. "I've brought you the man you requested."

Clabber motioned for Slocum to enter. He thought he had been transported to a different country—a different world. Elegant furnishings and artwork, both paintings and sculptures, were strategically placed throughout the entryway and the adjoining parlor room. Steps straight ahead went to the second floor.

As rich as the house was, the woman who greeted Clabber caused such material beauty to dim in comparison. Hardly five feet tall, she seemed larger, more dominant. Her finely boned cheeks and Roman nose were classical. Ruby lips, full and sensuous, parted as if to kiss him. Instead, she spoke.

"You have some sensibility?"

"Severigne, please, would I bring you a barbarian?"

"You have before," she accused. A toss of her head took her mane of thick black hair out of her blue eyes. She studied Slocum like he was some kind of bug and she was considering whether crushing him was worth getting the sole of her shoe dirty.

"Ma'am," Slocum said, tipping his hat to her.

"He should take off the hat in this house, but he has some notion of proper manners. I might have to instruct him."

"How lucky for him," Clabber said.

The two bantered, as if Slocum weren't there. He looked around and saw a woman peering around the banister on the landing. As if his mere sight could harm her, she squealed and disappeared. A few seconds later he heard whispering, quickly followed by feminine giggling. More than the one timid fawn resided above.

It didn't take Slocum much to figure out this was a whorehouse—a high-class one from the furnishings and the way the madam acted. But Clabber had been right about one thing. Keeping Severigne happy would certainly be worthwhile if she would only grace him with a smile. Her beauty was enough to take away his breath.

And he had thought of going to San Francisco to find lovely women.

"So?" Severigne said. "Has he explained all to you?"

"How is it you ended up in Clabber Crossing?" Slocum asked. "A woman as pretty as you ought to be back East, moving in society circles."

"So," she repeated, but this time with a different inflection. "Mr. Clabber has found a primitive with a spark of chivalry."

"I'm only saying what's on my mind," Slocum said. "And no, he hasn't told me what I'm to do for the next month, but I can guess."

"Can you? I doubt it," she said brusquely.

"You need a bouncer to keep order since the rodeo's coming to town. He doesn't mind the cowboys busting up his saloon, but he's got a special fondness for keeping this place intact."

"It is a brothel that I run," Severigne said. "And I *run* it. No ship on the high sea has a sterner captain."

"See what I mean, Slocum? You'll want to keep her happy or she'll give you twenty lashes."

"Only if he is very good," Severigne said. A hint of a smile danced on her lips. It faded as quickly as it was born. "You will keep order in the house. You will not cause any disruption or I will kill you."

"Sounds fair enough," Slocum said, "but why do you need me if you're able to, as you say, keep order?"

Severigne snorted and waved him off.

"You will sleep out back. You will know the place."

Slocum looked to Clabber, who nodded then bent over and gave Severigne a light peck on the forehead. The madam reached up, threw her arms around his neck, and planted a long, lingering kiss full on his lips. Slocum tried to figure out what was going on since Clabber looked a mite pissed, only there was something else mixed in. There was more than a hint of lust, but he did nothing to take Severigne up on what had to be a blatant invitation to go up to her bedroom for an afternoon of amorous exploration.

"You know how to discombobulate a man," Clabber said, sighing. "I'll have your horse and gear sent over, Slocum. Get to work right now since the Circle Bar boys are due in anytime now."

Severigne watched Clabber leave, further confusing Slocum. She had been exuberant with her kiss, but there was a touch of contempt in the way she watched the man's back. More went on under the roof of this cathouse than Slocum wanted to think on right now.

"There," Severigne said suddenly, pointing out the window. "They come. You will stay inconspicuous. No gunplay unless it is necessary. If they get too rough with the girls, you can do what you want to them, but don't kill them."

"Unless it's necessary," Slocum said, testing his limits. Severigne shrugged and hurried to the door to greet three cowboys. Unbidden a half-dozen soiled doves came down the stairs, mostly dressed. Slocum saw more than a flash of ankle. One had a slit cut in her dress that went all the way to her thigh and showed she wasn't wearing anything underneath. They lined up, flirted with the cowboys until they made their decisions, and then led the men upstairs.

"See? It is no different here than elsewhere," Severigne said.

"You've got a lot prettier girls," Slocum said, "than most brothels." He looked square into her bright blue eyes and said, "There's something else, too. The madam's a powerful lot prettier than any of her girls."

Severigne waved him off but was obviously pleased.

Slocum spent the rest of the afternoon doing nothing. Severigne greeted her customers and the ladies took care of the rest. The only trouble he had was with one cowboy not wanting to leave.

"They do not stay the night. Ever," Severigne told Slocum. And he took care of the problem, leading the cowboy out back and explaining to him how it was better to come back later and try a different lady of the evening.

He sat on the back porch and watched the stars wheel around as laughter and moans of pleasure came from the upstairs. Nothing had been said about him partaking of the services of any of the women, but Slocum had lost everything in the poker game. He wondered if Clabber might be talked into giving him a few dollars. For all that, he wondered if he had to pay for his own food. The place out back had proven to be a small house, sumptuous by his standards. It had been a month since he'd stayed in a hotel back in Denver, and he had shared the mattress with more fleas than he could count. Some of the bites were just now disappearing from his tough hide.

Severigne ran a clean establishment, and the bed in her guest house was downright comfortable.

"Slocum! Slocum!" Severigne's anguish was obvious. He took the steps up the porch and into the kitchen to find her clutching her throat with one hand and waving the other about in a manner that struck him at odds with her usual command. Severigne seemed lost.

"What is it?"

"It is Anna. Upstairs. I—"

Slocum shot past, took the steps up the back staircase two at a time, and found the other women clustered around an open door. He pushed through and saw what had unnerved Severigne.

The woman on the bed was obviously dead. She had spilled a full water glass, but he guessed this was not a natural death. Anna had not choked to death. He saw the brown bottle of laudanum on her bedside table.

It was empty.

2

"This is terrible," cried Severigne. "It cannot have happened." She pushed past Slocum, stared at the dead prostitute, then spun and shooed the others away. She kicked the door shut, leaving her and Slocum alone in the room with the body.

"You want me to get a doctor? Or the undertaker?" Slocum asked. These were not matters that suited him, but he had seen many dead bodies in his day—too many. Some were even lovelier than Anna, although the expression on her face went a considerable way toward erasing any hint of beauty that had been there. Her rouged cheeks looked obscene against the gray pallor of her skin. She had died in some pain from the look of her body and expression.

"Anyone hear her? I don't know much about opium but there might have been a chance of saving her if—"

"She did not kill herself," Severigne said unexpectedly. "Someone, someone did this to her. This is terrible!"

"What makes you think Anna didn't kill herself?" Slocum looked around the small, neat room. Other than the empty laudanum bottle and the spilled water the woman had taken it with, nothing was out of place. "Nothing's been disturbed."

"Oh, she was not robbed. The girls do not keep valuables in their rooms. They know better. What she owned, I have in the bank safe for her."

"If she wasn't robbed and there doesn't seem to be any sign of a fight, why—?"

"She was engaged to be married," Severigne blurted out.

"Might be she didn't cotton much to the man. Was it an arranged marriage?"

"No, nothing of the sort. Her fiancé came here from San Francisco. He is a rich man, a railroad magnate. He and Clabber had business dealings about shipping cows. Anna met him, quite by accident since he had not come to this house, and it was love at first sight." Severigne pursed her lips, kissed the tips of her fingers, and made a grand gesture. "I have seen such a connection between two hearts before."

"Maybe he found out what she did and broke it off?"

"He knew. Clabber told him. They are business partners. It would have been wrong not to. That did not matter."

Slocum looked around for a letter or some other indication that Anna had been spurned. He didn't find anything.

Shaking his head, he said, "She killed herself. There's no sign anyone was here."

Severigne stamped her foot and crossed her arms as she glared at Slocum.

"This is not so. Something happened. She was killed. You will find what became of her. That is now your job."

Slocum poked around the room and frowned. He ran his hand over the windowsill and it came away with a smear of blood. Wiping it on his jeans, he looked over the rest of the window. The smear came from the inside, as if someone with a wound had opened the window to get away. Outside on a ledge he saw another smear of blood and a piece of cloth caught on a splinter in the fancy wood facade. He pulled it loose and rubbed it between his fingers. It hadn't been outside very long since it wasn't dirty or weathered.

"What have you found?" Because of her agitation, Severigne's accent was almost too thick for Slocum to understand. Unlike many "French ladies," Severigne seemed to actually speak French natively.

"Who was her last customer?"

Severigne shrugged. She opened the door and spoke rapidly in French to a redhead out in the hallway.

"That is Alice," she said to Slocum. "She is so good at keeping track and I do not know what I would do without her. Anna did not have anyone last night."

"Her fiancé in town?" Slocum wondered if the rich man might have had second thoughts about marrying a whore and had taken the easy way out rather than letting Anna create a public scene.

"He is in San Francisco," she said. "I must wire him of this horrible tragedy."

"Wait a day or two."

Severigne looked sharply at him and said, "You see that she did not kill herself? Someone helped her do this thing?"

"Is that part of my job?"

"I say it is so a minute back. I will repeat this to you until you understand me. Clabber will say it is," she added, almost as an afterthought. "I must tell Clabber of this. It will cause such a scandal in town." She looked more distraught than ever.

Slocum continued to prowl around the room but found no other evidence to give him a trail to follow. Fresh blood. He went to Anna's body and examined her fingernails. He saw dark, dried blood under them. She had fought, but did she take the laudanum before or after? Anna might have another lover who didn't take news of her upcoming nuptials to another man well.

Slocum just couldn't tell—and he wasn't inclined to find out. If the town marshal cared, this was his job. Slocum wasn't so naive as to expect it to come raining down that way.

Alice stepped into the room and pointed at the body.

"She's dead, isn't she?"

Slocum said nothing.

"Anna's not the only one. There was another woman from town who died mysteriously a month back."

Slocum looked at Alice and finally said, "That's not so unusual. Life on the frontier is hard."

"You know Anna was murdered. I can see it in your eyes."

"That explains why I lost at poker," Slocum said. "Everyone reads my thoughts too quick." Alice's lips thinned and she started to angrily reply, but Severigne's return silenced her.

"The marshal is told. Clyde will know soon."

"The marshal's in his hip pocket?"

"No, not really. He pretends he is independent, but Marshal Dunbar is a fool. Clyde keeps him around for entertainment value more than law enforcement," Severigne said without rancor. Her statements were matter-of-fact, giving Slocum no chance to hear how she felt about the situation. From her looks, Severigne could make a brothel succeed wherever she went, but she had chosen to stay in a quiet cattle town in the middle of nowhere where the town's founder played power games to keep himself amused.

"Alice said another woman had died recently."

"Oh, she has so active the imagination. She should never listen to gossip." The more Severigne spoke, the more tortured her English became. He knew she was agitated but there must be more to Anna's death than she was telling him.

"What can you tell me about her railroad magnate?"

"There is so little to tell. They were in love. I have seen lust. I deal in lust. This was love. I know that, too." She turned her bright eyes on him. "Do not doubt me on this. Anna loved her Roy." She saw how he waited for more. "Roy Wilcox."

"I've heard of him. He's something of a recluse."

"Even the hermit must come out of the cave sometime. This one found love with my lovely Anna. My lovely, dead

Anna." Severigne stared at the body, then went to Anna and pulled the bedspread over her. She shivered and turned to go. Over her shoulder, she said, "You will find who killed this poor dove."

Slocum passed the corpulent undertaker coming up the stairs. The man smiled insincerely. If he had offered condolences, Slocum would have planted a fist on the tip of the man's dewlap-riding chin. Rather, the man continued walking up the stairs, gasping for breath by the time he reached the top. Slocum walked through the front door, Alice watching as he left. The undertaker removed the body just after first light. Slocum yawned and stretched, realizing he hadn't gotten any sleep at all.

He had to wonder at all that went on in this house. Shrugging it off since everyone saw more than a fair share of death and ugliness, he trooped along the double-rutted road toward town as the sun rose over the distant prairie. The saloon where he had lost his freedom for a month held no appeal to him, especially this early in the morning. Severigne kept cases of whiskey at the cathouse, and Slocum had been offered his share.

Although the Cross Timbers Saloon was a good place to listen to men talk, he doubted the cowboys would be doing much talking about a suicide in a saloon owned by the same man who owned the whorehouse. Besides, at this time of day anybody left inside would be hung over and moan more than talk. He doubted whoever had killed Anna would have stayed in town to drink himself insensate. From his experience in small towns, Slocum knew there were other places where such gossip would be rife. Slocum turned toward the general store as three women gathered near the door.

"Ladies," he said, touching the brim of his hat. He went inside but found some shovels just inside the door to linger over while he eavesdropped on the women a few feet away.

Word had spread fast. The undertaker had hardly returned to town with the body but the three women knew Anna's identity.

"Help you with a new shovel, mister?"

Slocum looked up. The store owner had watched him as he fingered the handle for several minutes.

"Nope, don't think this is what I need." Slocum left, heading out of the store so he could wander up and down Main Street. The quiet that had settled on Clabber Crossing gave him the cold shivers. The town felt as if it was getting ready for something terrible but didn't know what.

Slocum pushed such a thought out of his head. The only reason the town seemed this way was that he had a theory about a killer on the loose preying on women. Try as he might for the next few hours, he didn't overhear anything worth mentioning. The topic of Anna's death created a stir, but not that big a one.

Finding a dime stuck deep in his vest pocket, Slocum partook of lunch at another saloon, McCavity's, and asked a few tentative questions as he sipped his warm beer and gnawed on the tough beef in the sandwich. He might as well have been talking to a stone wall for all the response he got. Other than the fact that this saloon wasn't owned by Clyde Clabber, he found out nothing. He was the interloper and the local clientele wasn't inclined to share their thoughts with him. He finished his meal and stepped out into the hot afternoon sunlight. An entire day had been wasted on detective work, and he had no more idea about Anna's death than when he had started. He headed back toward the brothel.

"You're the newcomer," a man said from the shadows alongside the jailhouse as Slocum passed. He stepped out and sunlight caused his dull silver badge to gleam.

"You're the marshal," Slocum said.

"Reckon we're both something less than geniuses with those observations," the marshal said. "Mr. Clabber told me about you, said you were all right and would be working at Severigne's till the end of the month after the rodeo."

"Word travels fast," Slocum said.

"I'm not so sure you're all right," the marshal said. "Anna wasn't the kind to take her own life. I knew her."

"Professionally?"

"Of course," the marshal said without any guilt. "That's part of my job, keeping track of the ladies and collecting taxes on them." He cleared his throat. "If you mean, did I sample her goods, yup, did that, too. She was real pretty and had . . . skills."

"So you're looking into her death because it's personal," Slocum said.

"You might say that. You might also say I don't think Anna would kill herself like she did. She didn't use laudanum."

"How do you account for the bottle?"

"I didn't say others in the house weren't using that popskull shit. A newcomer to town wouldn't know that, now would he?"

"I had no reason to hurt her."

"Who knows what goes on when nobody's looking? She might not have wanted to share her bed with you, not with her getting ready to leave for San Francisco and a rich fiancé."

"That's a theory," Slocum allowed. "It's just not a good one." Slocum watched the marshal draw himself upright and rest his hand on the butt of his six-shooter.

"You got quite a mouth on you."

"You're not the first to notice. Who in town might have killed her—who might have had a real motive to kill her?"

"You don't know what you're talking about, Slocum, sayin' Anna had enemies," the marshal said. "You go poking around and bothering any of their families and I'll clap you in jail for disturbing the peace so fast your head will spin."

"Even if it means Clabber would get mad at you?" Slocum read the expression perfectly. He guessed that the marshal usually did as Clabber said—but wouldn't this time. There was a limit to Clabber's power and this was it.

"You get on back to your hole and crawl into it, Slocum. Don't go asking questions because folks in town don't like it."

"You don't like it. What if you're right that Anna didn't kill herself but was murdered? Solving that would be quite a feather in your cap, Marshal. It might make you eager to pin it on me because I've just come to town. Do that and you'll never find out what happened to her since you'll stop looking." Everything Marshal Dunbar said pointed to him wanting a quick and easy arrest and Slocum fit that bill perfectly.

"You got any wanted posters out on you, Slocum? Might take a while for me to go through the big stacks I have inside. Could be locking you up while I look through them would be in the best interest of town safety."

"No need. I'm on my way. If you want me, you know where you can find me. I'm crawling back into my hole." Slocum saw the combination of anger and fear mingling on the lawman's face. Before the marshal could think of a reason to arrest him, Slocum walked off, heading back in the direction of Severigne's whorehouse.

He didn't go far before he ducked down an alley and spent the next hour trying to overhear conversations or find out anything he could about Anna and the men who frequented her bed. Expecting to learn much this way was a fool's errand and Slocum gave up and finally did head back to the house. If he wanted to know any more, he would have to ask Clyde Clabber—but for some reason he was leery about doing that. Towns like this were run with an iron hand. Anything that happened in town had to be approved in advance, which meant Clabber knew as much about the woman's death as anyone. Slocum wondered if he could be responsible, though the motive for such a murder wasn't obvious.

A man as rich and powerful, at least in the region, as Clyde Clabber didn't need to kill a woman and make her death look like either an accident or suicide. He remembered how Severigne had acted around the town's founder. She and Clabber were partners in the cathouse. That much was obvious yet her concern for Anna was even more obvious. If Clabber had anything to do with Anna's death, Severigne would not cover it up. Or if she wanted to, why ask Slocum to find out how her soiled dove had come to meet her maker?

Slocum took his hat off to run his hand through his sweat-plastered hair. This saved his life since somebody was sighting in on his hat. He had it lifted six inches off his head and this was how much the bullet was off target. The hat went flying from his hand, and Slocum reacted instinctively by diving into the drainage ditch running parallel to the road.

He scrambled about, got his Colt Navy out, and cautiously chanced a look over the edge of the ditch.

The shot had come from a stand of cottonwoods ten yards on the far side of the road. He thought he saw movement in the gathering afternoon shadows but couldn't be sure. A six-gun against a rifle was no match, especially when he couldn't even be sure of his attacker's hiding place. He itched to jump to his feet and charge into the woods, firing as he went. Instead, Slocum remained still, watching the trees for any hint about his ambusher.

Ten minutes passed and Slocum finally crawled forward, retrieved his hat, and then advanced on the woods. The setting sun reflected off a spent brass cartridge on the ground. On a twig dangled a piece of cloth matching what he had found outside Anna's window the night before.

These were the only traces left by his would-be killer—and Anna's killer.

3

"This will not do," Severigne said, stamping her small foot. "I will not tolerate dirt in this house."

"Sorry," Slocum said, wiping off more mud from his jeans. Rolling around in the ditch half filled with water had not been the most sanitary thing he'd done in a while. What irked him as much as not finding who had taken the potshot at him was the hole in his hat. He used that hat to water his horse. Now, unless the horse went thirsty, he could only get a few ounces in the hat before the water sloshed through the two holes.

"Go, clean yourself. Do not expect me to send help. Do it yourself."

Slocum stared at her for a moment, then burst out laughing.

"That wasn't my intention rolling around in the mud." He held up the hat and poked his finger through the hole.

"What is this thing? You destroy your hat? How clumsy of you. Go, go." Severigne waved him away. Slocum noted her lack of understanding about what had happened. He had no reason to believe the madam wanted him dead. From everything that had happened, it was the opposite, yet he had wanted to see her reaction. She might be a good actress, but she had managed to feign complete ignorance of both his condition and the bullet hole drilled through the crown of his hat.

Evidence pointed to his ambusher trying to bushwhack him because he was trying to find Anna's killer. The tiny bit of cloth looked the same as he had found the night before, but this was hardly evidence that would convince a jury. All it did was make him warier and more alert for someone with a damaged coat. In a cow town like Clabber Crossing, worn clothing was the rule rather than the exception, but he could be on the lookout. Any smidgeon of evidence was better than what he had.

He left the kitchen and trudged to the shed behind the house. He saw a small stove for heating wood, a small stack of kindling beside it. It took a few minutes to get a fire started, but when he did, it felt good. The sun had sunk into the mountains far to the west and the air had turned cold. He shucked off his shirt and went to fetch water. Again to his surprise, there was a pump immediately inside the shed—or what he had thought was a shed. This was a bathhouse fitted with a large porcelain tub. Tables nearby held coal oil lamps and there was even a small wood floor inside to keep the patrons' feet from getting dirty, for Slocum knew that this was reserved for the paying customers.

The water had heated, but he only sloshed some of it on his hide to get off the worst of the mud. He stuffed his shirt and jeans into the water to clean them, then wrung them out the best he could and put on the wet shirt and jeans. Standing close to the stove dried them against his skin. It wasn't the best job in the world, but he was more presentable.

"Slocum!"

He dutifully returned to the house. Severigne's tone brooked no truancy, making him glad he hadn't bothered to heat enough water for a real bath. She would have caught him with his pants down for sure.

"There is some trouble. See to it. Be discreet. The one is an important man's son. But drunk, oh, he is so drunk."

"Gets mean when he drinks?" Slocum guessed. He read the answer by the set of the woman's jaw.

He took a small corridor that came out at the side of the parlor, where a man, not even out of his teens, held one of Severigne's Cyprians by the back of the neck. He forced her head down toward his lap. She struggled but was not strong enough to fight him off.

"Now, li'l lady, you jist go on and sample what I got to offer." He fought as much to get out the drunken words as he did to force the woman to his will.

"Now, little man, let's get some air," Slocum said. He caught the young man's wrist and turned it hard so he would release the woman's nape of the neck. She tumbled to the floor as Slocum's victim half stood and twisted, trying to escape the punishment given him.

"I'll horsewhip you. I'll horsewhip the two of you!"

Slocum leaned forward, tightened his grip, and felt bones in the wrist grating together. It would take only a little more pressure to break important parts—and the young man realized it. He stopped struggling. Slocum guided him back to a seated position on the sofa.

"You're a guest here," Slocum said in a low voice, "and you will act that way."

"I'm Martin Bray's son! You can't do this to me. I paid good money to get me a woman and—"

Slocum tightened his grip again.

"Keep your voice down. I was inclined to let you stay if you apologized to the lady—"

"What lady? Missy's a stinkin' two-bit whore!" The next sound from the man's mouth was a screech of pain as Slocum applied more pressure. Getting his feet under him, Slocum heaved. The young man followed. He had no choice. He would have had his arm broken off if he had resisted even an instant longer.

"I see that apologizing is out of the question." Slocum guided his prisoner along the hidden corridor and into the back of the house, where he heaved and sent the man stumbling.

The young man, lightning in his bloodshot eyes, turned and went into a gunfighter's crouch.

"I'm gonna cut you down where you stand."

"You won't be the first to throw down on me. You won't be the last either," Slocum said, standing easy, his hand at his side. He sized up his opponent. The threat was only a bluff. If he so much as twitched, Slocum would have his Colt out and would have two bullets in the man's heart before he could clear leather. He knew he could do it. He had done it before against men both faster and more sober.

The young man saw it, too.

"I'm Martin Bray's kid. He won't allow you to rough me up."

"Who's Bray?"

"He owns the bank, that's who he is. If I say so, he'll foreclose on this rat trap of a house and then all the whores will be sitting naked out along the road."

Slocum saw that the boy spun fantasies, both about what power his father had and what was likely to actually happen. If the bank owned the mortgage on Severigne's house of pleasure, the banker would be a fool to foreclose. Shutting down such a lucrative venture went against everything a banker believed in. More than that, if it came down to a couple of bull elks banging antlers, Slocum thought Clyde Clabber was more likely to win. A man like that had his finger in every pie. A bank was too obvious to ignore for a man who seemingly owned everything in sight.

"Do us both a favor and skedaddle. I don't want to fill you full of holes and I doubt anyone else does, even the lady you treated so bad inside."

"Missy wasn't no lady. She—" The young man stopped talking when he realized he was only digging his own grave if he kept up his bad-mouthing. He slowly straightened and moved his hand away from his holster. "Don't go doin' anythin' you'll regret," the banker's son said.

"That's good advice. I hope you take it, too."

The man backed away, then turned and stumbled off into the dark. Slocum had hardly returned to the kitchen when he heard loud voices coming from the front. He ignored Severigne's orders about being discreet and bulled his way through a small crowd of men and half-dressed demimondes to the front door, where a pair of cowboys scuffled.

He threw his arms around the pair of them and carried them off the porch and down the stairs. Turning, he released them so they both flopped onto the ground.

"Gentlemen, you can't have such noisy differences in this house."

"He was gonna take Mara. I wanted her tonight!"

"You had her last time. Mara's the best damn hooker in town."

"I'm sure she is desirable, but you two can't disturb the others. Settle your dispute or leave."

"You can't make us. We paid our money already."

"Both of you?"

The two cowboys nodded.

"Might be you could both see her."

"We gotta be back at the ranch by midnight. There wouldn't be time. Besides, who'd go first? Not him!"

"There would be plenty o' time if she started with you. You'd only need a minute. Me, I'd need the full two hours and—"

The two began wrestling. Slocum grabbed their collars and pulled them apart.

"I have a suggestion. I am sure Miss Mara would consider both of you at the same time." The suggestion took a few seconds to soak in. After all, if they both paid, that meant Mara could double her money for the time with the pair.

"She'd do that? I mean how'd that work?"

"A skillful courtesan such as Miss Mara would have to show you, but only if you cooperated." Slocum had piqued their curiosity and ignited their lust for the woman again. He led them back in, took Mara aside to explain, and after a little convincing, the dark-haired woman led both men upstairs, her arms hooked through theirs, one on either side, bumping hips as they went to the second floor.

"You are quite the innovator, eh?" Severigne said. "You convinced her by the twice money, yes? How did you get the cowboys to agree?"

"It gets mighty lonely riding the range," Slocum said. "It wasn't hard to talk them into it at all since they have to be back at work around midnight."

"Good," Severigne said, all business again. "You must lead a guest to the room at the rear of the upstairs. All lights are off. You will carry a lamp, turned low, so only he can see that he is going to the proper room."

"Doesn't want his identity known?" Slocum guessed.

"But no. He is influential and afraid for his position if he is seen here. Utter discretion is needed if you catch sight of his face, but you will not. He is a careful man in all ways."

Slocum went to the back door and lit a small oil lamp, put it on a ledge, and waited. Before long he saw movement in the darkness. The figure was heavily cloaked by a duster that dragged along the ground, and he had his hat pulled down so his face was hidden. Slocum wondered if this was necessary since he didn't know anyone in town.

"Good evening," Slocum said, picking up the lamp. The man jerked and looked as if he was going to run off. Slocum decided speaking was out of the question, so he opened the door but didn't hold it for the man. The kitchen was dark.

Slocum went directly to the stairs going up to the second story, taking the steps slowly. He heard the man following. Without turning, Slocum went to the end of the darkened hallway and opened the proper door. He went inside and kept his face turned as the man entered. Slocum left, taking the lamp with him.

"Stop. Leave the light."

"Sorry," Slocum said, almost laughing. He placed the lamp on a table and left, closing the door behind him. The hallway was pitch-black now so he had to feel his way to the head of the stairs. Only a faint reflection of light off a spoon left on the kitchen table below warned him he was getting close to the top step.

He kept the shiny spoon in sight as he went down the stairs carefully and finally stepped onto the kitchen floor.

From the front room he heard sounds dying down and then the front door closed. He wondered who it was that serviced the man upstairs. For all he knew, it might be Severigne. The man acted like a big shot so it stood to reason the madam herself would take care of his needs.

Slocum went to the parlor and sank onto the sofa. The women had gone to their rooms, presumably to sleep after a long night of entertaining. He tried to figure out how much money had changed hands that night and slowly drifted to sleep doing so.

The smell of burning wood made him come awake.

Like a racehorse out of the gate, he ran for the front door and flung it open in time to see a dark figure running away. His Colt Navy came into his hand as if by magic and he fired four times. He was sure three shots missed but wasn't certain about the fourth. Then there wasn't time to think about going after the man. Smoke curled up from the side of the house.

He ran around and saw flames licking hungrily against the wood. He whipped off his coat and used it to smother the fire. Then he stepped closer and began kicking pieces of wood away. Sparks shot into the sky, and grass around the house ignited. He kept swatting at the flames with his coat until his arms ached, but the house was in no further danger. He couldn't say as much about the grass.

It had dried out and now burned over a wide front.

"What's going on?"

"Alice, get the others. I need water. Lots of it to put out the fire."

He thought he'd have to repeat the order to the girl but she vanished into the house and within minutes five of the women emerged, mostly undressed, but all carrying buckets of water. From the back of the kitchen he heard the leather sucker washer on the pump working to draw up water. They formed a bucket brigade and in less than ten minutes only smoldering grass remained.

"What has happened?" Severigne came out, a robe pulled around her. Slocum explained how someone had tried to set fire to the house. "So you winged him?"

"Probably," Slocum said.

"Do not stand here. Hunt him down! Like a mad dog, hunt him and kill him!"

"Be sure to look for any embers that might—"

"Go, go," Severigne said, pushing him. "We will look. Alice has sharp eyes to see these things when I cannot."

Slocum went down the path toward the road, then cut back to the spot where he thought he had winged the arsonist. He dropped down to his knees and looked along the ground. A smile crept to his face after a few minutes of searching. Grass had been tromped down and was now only beginning to pop up again.

It took another half hour to find a drop of blood, looking black as ink in the light from the half-moon. He found a second drop and had a line to follow.

He was a good tracker but finding the man who had tried to burn down the brothel wasn't likely to happen. Not in the night. Slocum got halfway to town and then stopped and used his head. Once in town, the man could go anywhere. Most likely he would go to the town doctor if he was wounded seriously enough. If it was only a crease, hardly more than he might get off a splinter, the man would never be found. There probably wasn't a man in Clabber Crossing that didn't sport some kind of injury like that. Being a cowboy was rough work.

He glanced into the saloon as he passed but it was quiet inside. Slocum kept walking until he found the doctor's office upstairs over a barbershop. He started up, then hesitated and looked hard at the wood steps, hunting for any drop of blood that would be a giveaway.

He hadn't expected to find any blood and he didn't. Still, this was about the only lead he had. He tromped up the steps and knocked on the door to the doctor's office. He heard grumbling inside and then the door was flung open.

"What do you want?" The doctor stood a few inches shorter than Slocum's six feet and was wrapped in a black duster. When the doctor got a good look at Slocum, he tried to slam the door. Slocum kept it open by pressing hard against the wood panel.

"Has anyone needed attention for a bullet wound tonight?"

"Bullet wound? No, no one. Go away. You don't need medical attention." The doctor leaned against his side of the door. Slocum let him slam it, then took a half step back.

He might not have found the man who tried to set fire to Severigne's house but he had learned the identity of the mystery man who sneaked in under cover of darkness for a midnight tryst.

Slocum spent the next half hour futilely hunting for the arsonist before heading back to Severigne's.

4

"You can hardly see where the fire scorched the side of the house," Slocum said, stepping back and studying where the arsonist had plied his trade. He reached down and picked up a button, probably torn from the firebug's coat when he ran. Then again, with so many men coming and going at Severigne's house, the button might have lain in the dirt for weeks.

He held it up and turned it over slowly. It had come off an expensive coat and showed no signs of weathering, other than part of it being scorched. He pocketed the button. From the condition, it might have been ripped off, then heated by the fire after it fell to the ground. For all he could prove, the doctor had lost the button on one of his mysterious nocturnal visits to Severigne. Or any of the visitors to the house, but Slocum wondered about the young man who had tried to rough up Missy.

"No good, no," Severigne said, shaking her head and waving her hands expressively. "It must be painted over. Whitewash it. Do it now. Before this night when guests arrive."

"I couldn't track the owlhoot who set the fire, but I'm

sure he got on a horse and rode into town. The blood trail led in that direction."

"You have done all you could. I have spoken with Marshal Dunbar on this matter."

"He didn't take kindly to poking around and looking into who might have set the fire," Slocum guessed. From Severigne's sour expression, he knew he was right. "Is there much that the marshal does do in this town?"

"He is caught between powerful forces."

"That sounds like he's bought and paid for by two different men. Clabber? Who else?"

"The bank owner, Bray." She made a noise like a donkey, then kicked up her heels mimicking a balky pack animal.

"I take it you and him don't see eye to eye." Slocum slowly got the way power broke down in Clabber Crossing. Clabber might own damned near everything but he obviously didn't control the bank. Such a source of power was undoubtedly used to undermine Clabber at every turn.

"I would poke out his miserable evil eye," she declared. "I ask for the loan, he say no, I am a hussy and a poor business risk. Unless I put his lollygagging son in charge."

"What's the boy's name? He's the one I tossed out last night for roughing up one of your girls."

"Missy, yes, she told me. She would have accommodated Randall."

"Randall?" Slocum snorted. "Randy Randall Bray. Anyone call him that?"

"Not and live to speak it again," Severigne said. "He is a back shooter. He . . ." Her voice trailed off and her eyes grew wide. "You run him off after he hurt Missy. He is the one who tried to burn down the house!"

"Could be," Slocum said. He actually wished it was Randall Bray since he had taken an instant dislike to the boy. Seeing him rotting in the town jail would be sweet revenge. Otherwise, Slocum knew he would have to put a bullet through the boy's head or risk getting shot in the back.

If Randall Bray was the one who had tried to set fire to the house. If. He had no real proof. To reassure himself he might have something solid, he thrust his hand into his coat pocket and ran his fingers over the rim of the button. The spot where it had been closest to the fire was a little melted out of shape. This had come off an expensive coat, and while Slocum couldn't remember what Bray had worn the night before, it was more likely the ne'er-do-well son of a banker had lost it than some cowboy fresh off the range.

"I'll fetch some whitewash to take care of the burn marks," Slocum said.

"Tell Mr. Aronson to put it on my bill. He is a good customer, but do not mention this in front of his wife."

Slocum understood. Most of the men in Clabber Crossing came by at some time to sample the fleshy wares Severigne offered. He wondered what deal Clyde Clabber had. From the few seconds he had seen Severigne and the man together, he couldn't tell who called the shots. Clabber was a powerful man locally, yet he had deferred to Severigne.

"You need anything from the doctor?" Slocum watched Severigne closely. She would have made a good actress—and he wouldn't want to play poker against her. Only a tiny hint of surprise lit her face when he mentioned the shrouded visitor from the night before.

"You do not pry there, Mr. Slocum. There is a balance in this town that must not be upset."

"Why's he sneak over?" He thought for a moment and then said, "He's beholden to the banker, isn't he? What's Bray's hold on him?"

"Dr. Tarkanian is a man of too many vices. Women are only one."

"Gambling?"

Severigne nodded.

"So he's in hock up to his earlobes to Bray and doesn't dare show he even comes near a place owned by Clabber."

"I own this house." Her adamant tone told Slocum there was no point in poking for more information. He had enough in his head to confuse him now. Everything would sort itself out if he kept quiet, listened, and considered how it all fit together. Clabber Crossing had seemed a quiet little prairie town that lived off cattle ranching. Part of that was true—the part about raising cattle.

He was coming to understand that under the quiet surface boiled a sea of trouble.

The walk into town was spent turning over in his head all the possible problems he faced if Randall Bray was to be brought to justice. Chances were good he had done more than try to set fire to Severigne's house. Anger so uncontrolled had to vent in other ways. Who had died?

Slocum stood a little straighter when he thought of Anna lying across her bed, dead from the laudanum. Although he didn't know many people in Clabber Crossing, Bray was at the head of the list for killing the young woman. A moment of rage was all it would take. Slocum wanted to know if Randall Bray had scratches on him from a fight with Anna—and did he have a button missing on a fancy coat?

Setting a fire suddenly seemed like a minor crime in comparison to what the man might have done. And Anna wasn't the only woman to die in Clabber Crossing in the past couple months. Putting a round through Bray's heart might end a string of murders.

But Slocum had no proof. None. Yet.

"You Aronson?" Slocum called to the man wearing the apron sweeping the boardwalk in front of the general store.

"Sure am, and you're the fellow who can't decide what kind of shovel to buy."

"Made my decision."

"The long-handled one?"

"A gallon of whitewash."

For a moment Aronson stared at him, then laughed.

"In my day, men were picky. T'ain't so anymore, so I'm glad to see you've thought on it and come to a decision I can help you with. Come on in."

"Does it come in any other color than white?"

Aronson looked again at Slocum and saw he was joking. The shopkeeper slapped Slocum on the shoulder and said, "You got quite a sense of humor. That's been lacking in these parts. Glad to see someone's not going around all grim and determined."

Slocum followed Aronson into the store. He waited as the man barked orders to his clerk, then went to help. A woman wearing a sedate bonnet stood at the yard goods counter, running her hands over some gingham spread out in front of her. She cast sidelong glances at Slocum but never met his direct gaze. The longer she stood there, the more nervous she became.

He tried to get a better look at her face, but she turned as skittish as a colt and hid her face effectively, using the bonnet to that purpose.

"It'll take a few minutes to whip up," Aronson called. "My idiot son's got a lot to learn about keeping a good inventory."

"I'm in no hurry," Slocum said.

"Well, sir, you can just go on and look over them shovels to your heart's content." Aronson laughed at his joke and returned to the back room to get the whitewash ready.

Slocum ignored the shovels and went to a small case holding paintbrushes. He should have poked through the storage shed to see what tools Severigne already had, but buying a big brush now would save him a second trip into town if she lacked such a basic tool. More than that, he doubted Severigne cared what he put on her bill as long as he finished the chores she assigned.

The woman turned, looked down at the floor, and started past Slocum. She kept her eyes averted but her hip bumped into his—intentionally.

"Sorry, ma'am," he said. "I shouldn't be so clumsy." He reached up to touch his hat brim, but she caught his hand and held it in both of hers.

"My fault. Excuse me." She rushed from the store.

Slocum opened his hand and found a small square of

paper she had pressed onto him. He started to open it, but Aronson returned with the gallon can of whitewash.

"Got what you need right here. I see you're looking over them brushes. Interest you in one? And a shovel?" He laughed again at his joke.

"That brush," Slocum said. He turned and looked out the door. The woman hurried directly across the street, still in view. She looked back, distraught when she caught his eye. Then she ran off. "And some information. Who was that woman just in here?"

"The one looking so fondly at my fabric? She's off limits," Aronson said. "That's Emily Dawson. Mrs. Dawson, the new pastor's wife."

"Do tell." Slocum slid the paper into his side pocket. "Put this on Severigne's bill," he said, holding up the whitewash and brush. When Aronson hesitated, Slocum asked, "Anything wrong? She behind in paying?"

"Oh, nothing like that." Aronson looked around. "I just wanted to be sure the missus didn't overhear. She don't cotton much to Severigne, if you take my meaning."

"Reckon I do," Slocum said, lifting the can and tucking the brush into his pocket.

"You need anything more, you come on back." In a lower voice Aronson said, "Tell Severigne howdy for me." He looked around again to be sure his wife hadn't overheard, but she was nowhere in sight.

"Come on by anytime," Slocum said, enjoying the look on the merchant's face. It seemed Severigne serviced every man in the town, with the possible exception of Martin Bray, and Slocum wasn't sure about him. His son had no problem stopping by for a quick roll in the hay—or in his case, a little abusing of the soiled doves.

He stepped out into the bright Wyoming sun, pulled his hat down to shade his eyes, and looked around the town. He might be wrong but it seemed quieter than it ought to be. He had seen prairie dogs that'd pop up so far to the horizon that they couldn't be counted. Let a coyote come padding by and all the furry brown heads would disappear into their holes. This was the way Clabber Crossing felt to him—and he was the coyote.

Slocum started back to the house, then went to a shady spot where he could set down his can of gurgling whitewash for a moment. The scrap of paper unfolded several times. He saw how precise each fold had been. Emily Dawson was a methodical woman. The tight, crabbed writing reinforced this attitude. He held up the sheet to better decipher what she had written.

He read through it a second time, frowning. What could a pastor's wife have to say to him? And in secret? She wanted to meet out back of her husband's church, at an abandoned house. Slocum pulled out his pocket watch, the one that had once been his brother Robert's and now was his only legacy, and flipped open the engraved gold lid. Mrs. Dawson had asked him to meet her in about an hour.

A quick look at the sun told him it was going to get mighty hot this afternoon. It wouldn't be pleasant painting over the scorch marks, though the heat would dry the paint fast. He could avoid being in the worst of the sun by finishing the chore this morning, but it would take him longer than an hour to go back to Severigne's, paint, and then clean up before the evening customers started lining up.

Slocum came to a quick decision. His long legs devoured the distance to the house, but once there he did nothing to start painting. The whitewash and brush were stowed under the back porch. He hitched up his gun belt, got his bearings, and cut across a field, heading for a stand of pines. As he hurried along, he had to smile. This was the way the doctor had come in such utter secrecy the night before. When Slocum got to the stand of trees, he saw a small road winding through it.

If he explored enough, he would find every back road and secret way men from Clabber Crossing had to reach Severigne's house of ill repute. The road proved the exact route he wanted, coming out not too far from the doctor's office and running up a low hill to where the church stood. The steeple gleamed in the sunlight and the church doors stood open to catch some of the breeze beginning to blow away the heat. Slocum considered entering to see if the preacher was there, then changed direction and circled the base of the hill. As Emily Dawson had detailed, the pastor's house was some distance from the church itself. Slocum found a dirt path leading away from it and decided this was the right direction to find the deserted house she had mentioned.

Every step fed his curiosity. He was a newcomer to town. Why would a woman who was upstanding and, from Aronson's comment, seemingly devoted to her marriage want to see him? She knew nothing about him other than he was a drifter and worked at a whorehouse because he had lost a hand of poker.

Slocum stopped when he caught sight of the tumble-down house. It had seen better days. From the way the roof had collapsed into the house, he suspected too much snow was the culprit piled up on a roof that didn't slant enough. The walls bowed a mite and the single window on this side had been busted out.

He whirled, hand going to his six-shooter when he heard a horse neigh from somewhere behind him. Try as he might, Slocum couldn't see a rider or where the horse might be tethered. The preacher's house was out of sight around the hill and only the top of the church steeple poked up enough to see. From there it might be possible to keep watch on this house—but who would bother?

Still, a cold knot twisted his stomach. He had the feeling of eyes on him and couldn't find where anyone could lie in wait, spying. More cautious now, he went to the side of the house and peered through the broken window. When he saw nothing of interest, he moved to the only door into the cabin. The door had been removed, probably for use on a better house elsewhere. Even the brass hardware had been ripped from the wood frame.

"Mrs. Dawson? You in there? This is Slocum. You wanted to talk to me."

In the distance a bird chirped, but the house was silent. Other than the rising wind, he heard nothing. He poked his head inside, hand still resting on his six-gun. Slocum caught his breath when he saw the dark-haired woman sitting at a dusty table to one side of the room.

"Mrs. Dawson?" he called again, but he knew she wasn't going to answer him. She was slumped back in the chair, her head canted at an uncomfortable angle. Her breasts did not rise and fall with steady, easy breathing. Slocum didn't have to be a doctor to guess the reason for such stillness was the bullet hole in her temple.

On the table lay a derringer.

He went to her side and pressed his fingers into her throat, just to be certain. Her flesh was still warm, telling him she hadn't died too long before he showed up. It had taken him the better part of an hour to get here and she might have died anytime in that span.

Slocum spun, hand flashing to his six-shooter, but he didn't draw. He looked down the twin barrels of a shotgun pointed straight at his midsection.

"You're under arrest, but I'd as soon kill you where you stand, you murdering son of a bitch." Marshal Dunbar's finger came back on the twin triggers that would send Slocum to the Promised Land.

5

"I didn't kill her." Slocum knew he had only an instant to live. He was quick on the draw but could never clear leather, fan off a couple shots, and hope the marshal would miss with that room cleaner he held in shaking hands. At this range, half his body would go flying and the other half would be reduced to bloody mist by the buckshot in those double barrels.

"She was a good woman. She didn't deserve to get shot down by the likes of you." Dunbar's finger didn't lighten up on the double triggers, but he didn't pull back any farther.

"The derringer on the table. That's probably what killed her. Not my six-shooter."

"Your gun," the marshal said, the muzzle of the shotgun darting away from its target in the middle of Slocum's chest to point at the derringer. "Mrs. Dawson had no call to carry a gun. Everyone in town loved her and her husband. God, they have a son. He ain't got a ma now, thanks to you, Slocum."

"I didn't kill her."

"What you doin' here then?"

Slocum knew better than to answer truthfully. How could

he explain that the preacher's wife had passed him a note, like a misbehaving kid in school, asking him to meet her in this ramshackle house? He didn't know what she wanted to say, and any speculation on his part would get him killed by the marshal. Dunbar wasn't inclined to even wait for a lynch mob from the expression on his face.

"I had the morning off. I got some whitewash for Severigne and decided to wander about town. I haven't seen much of it, came upon the church, and then saw this place."

"You think you're like one of them fancy ass tourists from back East, come to breathe the fresh air and take the waters? Clabber Crossing ain't no resort town. We're hard-workin' folks. And you upped and killed one of the best of us."

Slocum counted himself lucky that Marshal Dunbar hadn't killed him.

"I heard a horse as I came up to this house. Whoever killed her might have ridden away before I got a chance to see him."

The marshal snorted.

"That was probably my horse. It's tethered outside. And don't go muddyin' the water sayin' I killed her. Nobody'll believe that for a second, Slocum."

Slocum looked at Emily Dawson's body.

"From the look of it, she might have killed herself. She have any call to do that, Marshal? I didn't know her."

"She'd never kill herself," the marshal said, but Slocum saw his anger and surprise fading. If he hadn't been so outraged, Slocum would have thought the marshal had killed her and then tried to frame him. But that didn't add up. The marshal would have shot him on the spot, claiming he caught the killer—Slocum—red-handed. More than this, Slocum doubted the marshal was a good enough actor to feign such shock and outrage. The man had actually gone pale under his leathery, sunbaked face at the sight of Mrs. Dawson's body.

"You got a mystery," Slocum said.

"I don't have anything of the sort. I got you. You can say your piece in front of a jury. Come along." Dunbar backed from the room but kept Slocum covered, not giving him a chance to escape.

As Slocum turned to get through the narrow doorway, the marshal plucked his Colt from his holster and tucked it into his own belt.

"What were you doing out here, Marshal? You always take a ride this time of day sporting a shotgun?"

"You shut your mouth. What I was doin' out here's none of your damned business."

Slocum knew he had touched a nerve with the lawman, but he couldn't figure what it was. Mrs. Dawson didn't sound like the kind of person to have an affair with a grimy, smelly old cuss like the marshal. If she had a son, she would be far more discreet about any affair. Shuffle being married to the town pastor into the deck, and the cards simply refused to come up with anything Slocum could read.

"You going to let her body stay out here in the heat?" Slocum asked.

"You keep quiet. I'll get the undertaker out when I can. Lockin' you up is more important right now."

"I didn't do it," Slocum said.

"In all my years as a lawman, both deputy and marshal, I ain't never arrested a single man what wasn't innocent."

"I can believe that," Slocum said dryly.

"I mean, that's what they tell me. They were all as guilty as sin. You're gonna swing for this, Slocum. She was a good woman."

The marshal rode while Slocum walked back to the jail, where Dunbar shoved Slocum into the small calaboose. Two empty cells stood with doors ajar. Dunbar threw him into the nearest cell and slammed the door. With grim finality, the metallic click as the marshal turned the key in the lock told Slocum he was in a passel of trouble.

"Do I get a lawyer?"

"Only a couple in town. We had more but they got run

out on a rail. They was takin' money to throw cases. We got a fine prosecutor these days. I'm gonna let him know he's got a case to make against a real cold-blooded killer."

Slocum had hoped the marshal would leave, giving him the chance to get free from the cell. Right offhand he didn't see how he could escape, but he wasn't going to try if the marshal remained in the jailhouse. Instead, Dunbar opened the outer door and bellowed, bringing an urchin of seven or eight running.

"You go fetch Mr. Cooper for me, will you, Jed?"

"Mr. Cooper? Who's dead?"

"Don't you worry yourself none about that, boy. Fetch him." The marshal fumbled in his vest pocket. "Here's a penny. You get him back here double time quick and there's another one waitin' for you."

"Thanks, Marshal." The boy ran off as fast as his bare feet could take him.

Dunbar closed the door and half smiled, saying, "That boy's got a good head on his shoulders. All the time lookin' to make a nickel or two. One day he's gonna buy Clabber out, mark my words." Then Dunbar sobered and glared at Slocum. "But you ain't gonna see that day. You're gonna be buried six feet under out on Primrose Hill. Not on the top, if I got any say about it. No, I want your grave to be at the base of the hill. No reason you should have a decent view for the rest of eternity."

"Emily Dawson's likely to be planted higher on the hill," Slocum said. "You wouldn't want us together, would you, Marshal?"

"She—" Dunbar glared at Slocum, then dropped his shotgun on a battered, stained desktop and planted himself firmly in the chair behind the desk. "You don't go sayin' nothing bad about her."

"I wish she was alive," Slocum said. "Can I send word to Severigne telling her why I'm not whitewashing the side of her house?"

Stony silence greeted him. Slocum sank to the hard bed

and began his survey of the door, hinges, bars, wall, floor—he could get out but it would take him a considerable amount of effort. If he stayed under the marshal's watchful eye, there was little chance he could do anything to escape.

The jail became increasingly hot and Slocum lay back, ignored the bedbugs the best he could, and was dozing off when the outer door slammed open and rapid, clicking footsteps came in. Slocum looked up to see Severigne standing in front of the marshal, hands on her hips and looking like a prairie thunderstorm.

"You will release him now!" Severigne said.

"I can't go doin' a thing like that," Dunbar said. "He killed the preacher's wife."

"He did no such thing. You sent Lloyd Cooper to get her body."

"Of course I did. I ain't leaving' her to rot out in the summer heat."

"Lloyd says she killed herself. Why do you hold Mr. Slocum?"

"Cooper said that? Well, Slocum is a witness. He found the body and I don't want him runnin' off."

"I guarantee he will not."

"Got to post bail for him."

Slocum heard the crash as Severigne slammed her fist down and left behind a stack of greenbacks.

"You did not hear a shot, did you, Marshal?"

"What's that got to do with anything?" Dunbar looked increasingly uncomfortable.

"You would have heard the shot if Slocum had killed her. You did not."

"Look, Severigne, this—"

"Release him!" Severigne put one hand on her hip and pointed imperiously with her other hand, index finger stabbing in Slocum's direction.

"If you vouch for him." Dunbar poked through the stack of money and looked up. "You talk to the judge about this?" He read the answer in Severigne's dark look. The lawman heaved a sigh, pulled the key ring out of his desk drawer, and released Slocum. "Don't you think you're gettin' away scot-free, Slocum," the marshal grumbled.

"I didn't kill her. Why'd you throw me in jail for something you know I didn't do?"

"The banker demanded it," Severigne said. "Marshal Dunbar is beholden to Bray." She made her mocking donkey sound again.

"You don't go makin' them insultin' sounds, Severigne. I'll throw you in jail for disturbin' the peace, you keep that up."

Severigne smiled and the mockery was far worse than the donkey braying. Slocum said nothing more as he grabbed his gun belt and waited until he was outside to strap it on.

"You should have whitewashed my house, not go gallivanting off this way," Severigne said. Her French accent turned thicker again. Slocum wasn't sure if this was because she was madder at him than at Dunbar or if she was cooling off.

"Never thought I'd find a dead parson's wife while I was out walking around town," Slocum said.

Severigne started to ask the question needing most to be answered but held back. Slocum wasn't sure he could give a good answer to why he had bothered to meet Emily Dawson other than curiosity. She had been flustered and had taken time to pass him a note so no one else in the general store noticed. Whatever had sparked her note, it couldn't have been trivial.

Slocum pursed his lips as he wondered if it might have something to do with Severigne's cathouse. Had the young Mrs. Dawson worried her husband was partaking of the charms offered by Severigne's ladies? Who better to ask than a newcomer to town without all the political chains binding him to one faction or the other?

Still, she must have known his indebtedness to Clabber since about everyone else in town did.

"Two months," Severigne said.

"What?" Slocum stared hard at her, wondering what the hell she meant.

"You owe me another month. You owe Clyde a month. Now because of the money I pay that foolish marshal, you owe *me* a month."

"Sounds more like slavery."

"Pay me back the bribe money I give Dunbar and you are free."

"Wasn't it bail money?"

"Pah," Severigne said, waving her hand about in the air as if shooing away flies. "Bribe, bond, fine, there is no difference in Clabber Crossing. It freed you. More than this is something you should never ask for."

"If you don't mind, I've got an errand to run before I get back to your indentured servitude." This caused a slight smile to curl Severigne's lips. She came close to laughing.

"I understand this. He is in the church."

"Not much gets by you, does it?"

"Dunbar would never ask. You must since your neck is the one he wants to put into a noose. Go, go, question Henry Dawson." She went to her buggy beside the jailhouse and rattled off, impatiently flicking the reins to keep the horse moving in spite of the oppressive afternoon heat.

Slocum headed for the church and found the pastor in the front pew, head bowed and lips moving silently.

"Sorry to bother you, preacher," Slocum said, "but I wanted to pay my respects."

"Bad news always travels so fast," Henry Dawson said, looking up. His eyes were red from crying, and it took him a second to focus. "You must be the man who found her."

Slocum hesitated. The preacher wasn't accusing him. He didn't even seem to know who had been jailed for his wife's murder.

"The undertaker said he thought it was suicide. You have a family, a boy?"

"Yes, Edgar," Dawson said, nodding. He sat a little straighter. "This is going to be difficult for him. He had not wanted to move here from back in Kansas, but God's calling could not be denied."

"Was your wife agreeable about uprooting and moving?"

"Yes, Emily understood."

"How long have you been in town?"

"Less than two months. Six weeks," Dawson said.

"Did she have any reason to kill herself?"

Dawson jerked around and looked at the altar. His lips moved in silent prayer before he answered.

"Emily had a troubled past. We moved here to put that behind us."

"That and God telling you to come here."

"Not here specifically. We stopped traveling when we ran out of money. Clabber Crossing was the first town we found that was in need of spiritual ministry."

"You didn't know anyone in town when you came?"

"No one," Dawson said. "The folks in Clabber Crossing have welcomed us with open arms, but—"

Slocum waited. Dawson had started to say more and had forced himself not to. The silence lengthened into a minute—more—but Slocum remained quiet. He had been a sniper during the war and had learned the value of patience. It paid off again, not with a clean shot but with the preacher finally figuring out what he wanted to say.

"Emily was fine for the first week or so in town, but she grew increasingly restive." Dawson drew a deep breath before adding, "I could even say she was anxious."

"Any reason?"

"None that I could see. She had done well organizing a ladies' auxiliary. Edgar was fitting in. He has found several other boys his age I am sure he counts as friends now."

"So whatever caused your wife's upset happened a month or so back?"

"'Upset' is a strong word. Perhaps the heat wore her down. But I cannot believe it caused her to kill herself."

"That means she was murdered."

"Please go now, unless there is something more I can do for you." Dawson turned away, closed his eyes, and began a new prayer.

Slocum left, having learned nothing of real importance. Emily Dawson had begun fitting into the social whirl of Clabber Crossing, such as it was, and could hardly have made an enemy so quickly willing to kill her. That left suicide, which seemed to be of almost epidemic proportions in the small cattle town. Slocum couldn't get Anna's cold, lifeless body out of his head. Two women had died since he came to town, one by poisoning and the other by gunshot—and both might have been suicides.

A hooker's life, even working at a classy brothel like Severigne's, was difficult. Was a preacher's wife's existence equally difficult? If so, why hadn't she waited to meet him before shooting herself in the head? Why bother even writing the note and arranging a meeting with a stranger to town?

None of it made a whit of sense.

He started back for Severigne's. As he passed the restaurant, movement inside caught his eye. He stopped and saw a woman dressed in a red-and-white-checkerboard apron and a gingham dress waving a linen napkin at him.

"Ma'am," he said. "Is there something I can do for you?"

The woman, a slender blonde with eyes so blue they were almost transparent, pursed her lips, as if thinking over his offer. Then she said, "I'll close the café. Come around back."

"Beg your pardon?"

"Emily didn't kill herself. She couldn't have," the woman said. She shut the door in his face and flipped the sign in the window around. Slocum stared at CLOSED as he wondered what was opening up around back.

Cursing himself for a fool, he went to see.

6

Slocum looked around the dusty street but nobody stirred in the afternoon heat. He went down the narrow alley between the restaurant and the gunsmith shop next to it and saw where supplies were unloaded. He started to knock but the door opened before his knuckles hit the wood and the woman's slender fingers wrapped around his wrist and pulled him inside.

"I knew you'd come," she said breathlessly. The way her breasts rose and fell under the gingham dress distracted Slocum a mite. He wondered why since he had spent enough time in Severigne's cathouse to see his share of naked women darting about. But the blonde was different somehow. She was fully clothed—and something of a mystery. He liked that.

"I'm John Slocum."

"Sara Beth Vincent," she said, still breathing heavily. She moved a little closer to him and lowered her voice. "I can trust you, can't I?"

Slocum had to laugh.

"Doesn't much matter what I say to that," he answered. "If I'm a liar, I'll say you can. And how'd you know if I was an honest man saying that same thing?"

Her blue eyes stared into his green ones. He saw something change in the way she looked at him.

"I can tell you're honest. You give your word and you keep it."

"That wasn't a question," he said.

"It's the way you live your life. I see a lot of cowboys come and go through my café, and I've learned what's bullshit and what's not."

"Now that you've settled that in your mind," he said, "what is it you're trusting me to say or do?"

"Emily," she said, not moving away from him. "Emily Dawson. She didn't kill herself. She was afraid of something—of someone."

"Who might that have been?"

"She wouldn't say. She and her family'd only been in town six weeks or so, but she changed a month back. Before then, she was friendly and outgoing but she got increasingly morose."

"Enough to kill herself?"

"No!" Sara Beth reached out and grabbed Slocum's arm with surprising strength. "She would never do that and leave her son without a ma. And she loved Henry. Heaven alone knows why, but she did."

"Why do you say that? I was just at the church, and he's mighty tore up over her dying."

"He loved her, but he loved his church more. He'd ignore her to help a parishioner. If Edgar—that's their son—needed help, he was as likely to be ignored if there was a church fund-raiser or baptism on the calendar."

"Devoted," Slocum said. He was more interested in Sara Beth than in her tale about Emily Dawson.

"She wouldn't kill herself."

"I didn't kill her."

"I know," Sara Beth said, her eyes fixing on him again. "I've watched you around town. You're . . . dangerous." She licked her lips. "But you wouldn't murder a woman."

"The marshal doesn't think so."

"Dunbar is a fool," she said. Then she snorted and shook her head. A tiny halo of fine blond hair came loose and caught the sunlight filtering in through a side window, turning her angelic. "But it's more than that. He's owned lock, stock, and barrel."

"Banker Bray," Slocum said.

"You've figured it out. There are two factions in town. Clabber and Bray."

"Where do you line up?"

"With the truth, and I want to know what happened to my friend. Emily was a tormented soul, but she wouldn't kill herself. She lived for her boy and she loved Henry, no matter how he spent his time."

"Why are you telling me this?"

"I want you to find out what happened to her. It . . . it might be she killed herself. If so, that ought to be brought to Henry's attention why he was responsible, but if she was killed, the murderer ought to hang. I want to find out the truth."

"I'm not a lawman," he said with some distaste. The last thing he ever wanted to be was a marshal.

"But you have a stake in finding how Emily died. You find who really killed her and you're in the clear."

"I don't have trouble sleeping at night," he said.

"I didn't think so," Sara Beth said, moving closer yet so she pressed into him. "But sleeping isn't all you do in bed, not a big buck like you."

Slocum considered where he was employed and how he got nothing from it other than working off a debt of Clyde Clabber. Sara Beth's intentions were obvious to him. She wanted to make sure he found how her friend had died and was willing to seal the deal any way possible.

"It might take a while," Slocum said, reaching behind Sara Beth and unfastening her apron. It fell to the floor.

"Really? How long?" She worked to get his gun belt off and tossed it onto a nearby chair.

"Hard to say." He began opening the tiny pearl buttons

on her dress. When it fell open to her waist, he caught his breath. She didn't wear anything underneath. Her fine, firm breasts were exposed. He cupped them and gently massaged. Sara Beth closed her eyes, arched her back just enough to shove herself forward into his grasp a little more, and then shivered in delight.

"I don't mind if it's hard," she said. Her hand pressed into his belly and slid down to his crotch. "Ohhh!"

"It's getting harder," Slocum said. He caught his breath as she popped open the last button on his fly and let him come snapping out, long and steely and ready. Her fingers curled around him and began stroking.

"I noticed," she said. The blonde dropped to her knees in front of him and took his length into her mouth. Her lips closed around the tip and then she moved slowly forward. Slocum grunted as she began playing with the sac dangling beneath his shaft. He wanted more from her, but pushing the willing woman away was difficult.

She drew back, looked up at him, blue eyes sparkling, and said, "Is there anything else you'd like?"

"You're reading my mind," he said. He reached down and cupped her breasts, lifting upward to get her to her feet again. His hands slid down her sides, then sneaked under her skirt and ran along bare legs. She wasn't wearing any undergarments there either.

Sara Beth groaned softly when his finger entered her most private place. Her stance widened, but Slocum wasn't able to do more standing. His hands ran around behind and gripped her fleshy rear. He lifted in one smooth motion, her legs spreading and going on either side of his hips. Walking back a few steps, he deposited her on a table. She thrashed about, knocking things to the floor with a clatter. Slocum was too occupied to know what had been on the table. All that mattered to him was now perched on the edge.

Sara Beth lifted her feet and placed them on the table as she leaned back, supporting herself on her elbows. Slocum saw her breasts bob gently as she swayed about. Her knees parted even more as she scooted around to position herself for him. Slocum moved forward and found the target they both wanted hit. Hips moving slowly, steadily, he entered her.

The woman cried out as he sank balls deep into her tightness. He reached around and gripped her waist to keep her from sliding away from him on the table. Tiny puffs of white rose all around. She had been preparing something for the evening meal and the flour was now creating small clouds around her as she writhed on the table.

"More, yes, oh, yes, more, John," she sobbed out. She arched her back and shoved her hips toward him, taking him another fraction of an inch deeper.

Slocum reveled in the heat all around his manhood, but that clutching, moist interior worked on him. He felt pressures mounting deep within and had to move. His hips moved away, pulling him out of the snug berth, but he hesitated for only an instant before slipping back. He sped up his movements until he stroked as fast as any piston on a locomotive. Friction caused heat, and the explosion of desire within his loins was not to be denied. Faster he stroked and then he erupted, pulling the woman hard to him.

She lay back, hanging on to the edges of the table as she cried out. Her body shuddered and then she sighed, sinking to the table. Sweat beaded her forehead, and droplets between her breasts glistened like dew. Slocum bent forward and kissed them away.

"I didn't make a mistake," she said.

Slocum looked at her.

"You're a hard man to deny," Sara Beth said, laughing. "I'm glad you've agreed."

Slocum wasn't sure what he had agreed to, but was satisfied enough with the last few minutes. He stepped back, motion drawing his attention. From the corner of his eyes he had seen a flash at the window, but he saw nothing now. He buttoned up, strapped on his six-shooter, and then went to the back door.

"You're not going, are you, John?" Sara Beth Vincent

worked to get her blouse buttoned. "We have more to talk over."

"Just a minute," he said, stepping outside. Nobody was in sight. He went to the side of the restaurant and looked at the ground. The dust was too kicked up for him to get any idea if someone had been watching him and Sara Beth, but he looked closer at the edge of the window. A partial handprint in the dust there showed someone had pressed close, probably looking in, but not enough remained for him to know much about the Peeping Tom. He couldn't even say that this was a fresh print.

But he thought he had seen movement. Slocum wasn't inclined to imagine such things.

"John? Where are you?"

Slocum returned to the rear door, where Sara Beth waited anxiously.

"I thought you'd run off." She swallowed hard and added, "I didn't want to run you off. Quite the opposite of that." She moved closer, her now-clothed breasts pressing once more into his chest.

"Why are you so anxious to know about Emily Dawson?" he asked.

"We'd both just come to town. I arrived a month or two before her and her family. Getting to know anyone in Clabber Crossing without having to make enemies to match the friends is hard work. She and I were able to talk because we weren't part of either faction."

Slocum understood this.

"How'd you get the money to start this restaurant?"

Sara Beth's eyes took on a fierce look. She heaved a deep breath and finally said, "No thanks to Bray. He wanted more than I wanted to pay in return for a loan."

"So where'd the money come from? Clabber?"

"I got an inheritance," she said. Then, "Oh, all right. My husband died and left me a considerable amount of money. I used all of it to get the restaurant going." She saw his skeptical look. "Wyoming doesn't mind if a woman owns property," she said. "Who knows? A woman might be governor of Wyoming one day."

"You?"

"Oh, no, not me. I like fixing a pot roast and potatoes for an admiring clientele too much. And I make a great peach pie."

"Dessert is mighty good," Slocum agreed.

Sara Beth laughed delightedly.

"You are not a subtle man, John Slocum, but I don't mind. You can come by for dessert anytime you want, no matter where else you've had dinner."

"Only here, since I came to town," Slocum said. This seemed to startle Sara Beth. "I work for Severigne. Hired help's not allowed extra servings from the table."

"No breakfast in bed? I'm surprised."

"I've got work to do out there—whitewashing the side of the house."

"I heard that somebody tried to burn the whorehouse down."

"You and Emily shared a distaste for Severigne's business, didn't you?"

"I . . . yes." Something in the way Sara Beth answered put Slocum on guard, but he didn't pursue the matter. There would be time later. He gave her a quick kiss and then went back to Main Street, going down the alley where the window showed the part of a handprint that mocked him. He wished he knew more about who had spied on them in the back room—and why.

Out in Clabber Crossing's main thoroughfare, he saw a few people stirring. The worst of the afternoon heat was past, and the cooler evening would be along soon to allow more a more civilized conduct of business. From all Slocum could tell, the town sat in the middle of a dozen or more ranches. The cattle business brought a couple hundred horny cowboys into town, to drink and whore and kick up their spurs a mite to relieve the boredom of the range.

More than this, they needed supplies and the ranch owners needed bank credit and things only a town could supply. Clyde Clabber had a profitable mercantile center here, and from all Slocum could tell, Martin Bray had dealt himself into a profitable game.

Slocum licked his lips, thinking on how the cowboys came in for a taste of whiskey, but he had lingered in town long enough. He hadn't found any more about Emily Dawson's killer—or if she might have shot herself—but he had certainly found a mighty tasty meal over at the restaurant in the person of its owner. Sara Beth's image kept him happy all the way back to Severigne's house.

He poked around inside, hunting for the madam, but she was nowhere to be seen. Slocum went out back, rummaged under the porch, and got the whitewash and the new brush for the chore of painting out the scorch mark on the wall. About the time he had finished and had cleaned up a mite from where he had splashed the whitewash all over himself, he heard Severigne coming up in her buggy. He went out to see to the horse.

Severigne was already out and halfway to the house. She turned when she saw him and said, "You will stand outside this evening. No customers."

"Why not?"

"We have the special business inside the house."

"All the girls?"

"No exceptions. All, every one of them," Severigne said. She pointed to a stack of boxes piled in the back of her buggy. "Bring those. They will be needed this night."

Curious, Slocum went to the boxes and managed to pry open a corner of one as he picked up the box. Inside lay some frilly undergarment he couldn't quite recognize since it wasn't gracing some feminine form. From the weight of the boxes, all held clothing.

He put the pile down just inside the door. Severigne pointed and began instructing her ladies what to take. To Slocum, she said again, "You will chase off any customers this night."

"Even if they come in the back way?"

"All. This is important business, but not that kind of business." She made lewd thrusting motions with her hips, then yelled at one girl, who held up a corset upside down.

Slocum tended the horse and made sure the buggy was clean of dust and mud for the next time Severigne wanted to use it. Then he checked his six-shooter to be sure it rode easy in its holster before he went to the road to tell any customers that the house was closed for the night.

He thought there would be some trouble, and there was.

7

"Sorry, boys, Severigne's not taking any visitors tonight," Slocum said to a trio of drunk cowboys who'd ridden from the direction opposite town. Wherever they'd started drinking, it wasn't in any of Clabber Crossing's saloons. He bent down and picked up a small stone, clutching it in his right hand.

"You're quite a card, mister," the drunkest of the three said, almost falling from the saddle. "We done rode eight miles to come here. Our boss is a real hardnose when it comes to his crew gettin' some ree-lax-ation. Took 'bout ferever to talk him into lettin' us come to town."

"Go on into town. One of the saloons will be glad to accommodate you."

"We like Severigne's place. Real classy. We like classy whores, not them poxy two-bit bitches in town. Why, one of them at McCavity's Saloon damn near bit my nose off! We're goin' in and you ain't stoppin' us, no, siree."

"Give you twenty dollars to go on into town," Slocum said. "You might spend it or you might save a few dollars and come back here tomorrow for some first-rate fun." He had no idea why Severigne had closed for the night or if she might be inclined to open tomorrow. All he wanted was to get rid of the three cowboys. If they came back tomorrow and Severigne's ladies still had their legs crossed, Slocum could deal with the problem then.

"Now." For all the liquor he had poured down his gullet, the cowboy was remarkably adept with his six-gun. He had it out and pointed at Slocum quicker than he thought.

Slocum tossed the rock as hard as he could, striking the cowboy's horse on the shoulder. The horse reared. The cowboy fired but doing so from a rearing horse was hard and he was drunk. Slocum grabbed the reins, worked past the kicking front hooves, and grabbed a handful of the cowboy's shirt. With a huge tug he unseated the man and brought him crashing to the ground. For a moment, Slocum thought he had killed him. The cowboy lay unmoving. His two buddies started going for their six-shooters but the fallen cowboy groaned and pushed up to hands and knees.

"Wha' 'appened?"

"You had one hell of a fine time at Severigne's," Slocum said, dragging him to his feet and shoving him toward the skittish horse. "Now you're going into Clabber Crossing and whoop it up."

"I had a good time?"

"The best." Slocum shot a cold stare at the other two cowboys. Neither was drunk enough to cross John Slocum.

"Yeah, you had one fine tumble," one said. The other laughed and soon the trio was trotting toward town. Slocum stepped back, dusted himself off, and was grateful he hadn't had to pay the twenty-dollar gold piece he had promised. If he'd had that much, he'd buy his way free of this indentured servitude.

He grumbled as a buckboard rattled up from the direction of town. A solitary man drove and was inclined to go right past Slocum. Slocum caught the reins and stopped him.

"House is closed tonight," Slocum said. He hadn't been in town long enough to know everyone but a man this well dressed would have stood out. Even the banker's son hadn't sported such a fine coat.

"Madame Severigne is expecting me. I'm the reason the house is closed this evening."

"Do tell," Slocum said. He looked into the back of the wagon and saw several long packages wrapped in dark cloth. If they hadn't been so skinny, he would have wondered if this gent was bringing dead bodies to the brothel.

"You're not the undertaker, are you?"

This caused the man to look surprised, then laugh harshly.

"Mr. Cooper and I often share customers, but not in the way you imply. Now, let me go in. I will not keep Madame Severigne and the ladies waiting one minute longer than necessary."

Slocum considered holding the man here and asking Severigne, then decided to let him through. The buckboard rattled to a halt in front of the house and the man secured the reins and began working on the packages in the back. Slocum sauntered up and asked, "You want some help?"

"It is very fragile equipment. Do not break any of it or it'll come out of your pay!"

Slocum had to laugh at that. He was already stuck here for two months because he had no money. Whatever the man brought to Severigne's would probably run that sentence of service to years, if it was both as fragile as the man said and as expensive as Slocum guessed. He grabbed a package wrapped in black silk cloth and pulled it toward him. As he pulled it from the buckboard, he traced the outline of what was wrapped.

"You prospecting? This feels like a tripod for a surveyor's transit."

"You have a remarkable sense of feel. I am sure the ladies appreciate that." The man laughed, but there wasn't a trace of humor in it. He carried a large box himself and kicked at the door rather than setting it down and knocking.

"Monsieur Molinari, you are so prompt. Come in, come in," Severigne greeted the man. She held the door for her visitor but Slocum had to deal with getting inside on his own. He brushed aside the black cloth and saw his wild guess had been surprisingly accurate. He did carry a tripod.

Molinari pointed to a spot to one side of the parlor, and Slocum carried the tripod and set it up, holding the silk cloth, not knowing what to do with it. He finally tossed it to one of the half-clad girls, who grinned at him, lifted it coyly while showing one bare breast. She laughed, spun, and began using the black silk to hide strategic portions of her anatomy.

"April, stop that," Severigne snapped. "We are here to work, not to play. You will do as Monsieur Molinari says. No more, certainly no less!"

"Oh, very well, Severigne," the girl said, chastened.

Slocum stepped back into a corner, watching as Molinari set up his camera. The black silk cloth was a hood that draped over the rear of the large boxy camera. Several times Molinari ducked under it, reached around, fiddled with the lens, and then pulled out from underneath the black curtain and finally cast a gimlet eye not at April but the background.

"This will not do. Nothing so busy behind her. You want something simple, but no pictures. Nothing like that, like that or that." He flicked his wrist in the direction of the offending wall hangings.

"Well, Slocum, get them down. Do as he says. Now, now!"

Slocum almost laughed at Severigne's orders. She was obviously irked at Molinari telling her the fine paintings were not suitable as background for his pictures of almost naked women. He took them down and noticed the discolored wallpaper around the paintings. In spite of Severigne's constant housekeeping, the paper had faded where sunlight touched it, no matter how briefly in the late afternoon.

"That will not do either. Must I do everything?"

"Andrew, a word," Severigne said, taking Molinari's sleeve and pulling him to the foot of the stairs.

"I'm glad I'm not the one getting that tongue-lashing," April said. "Unless you want to give it to me, John." She bumped a bare thigh against him and smiled coquettishly.

"I haven't seen him around town," Slocum said. "He just come here?"

"Six months back, maybe longer. He travels around the countryside a lot," April said. "He takes photographs of families for the ranchers. Cracked Tooth Harry Bennett had him take pictures of all his cowboys. Said it was going on a wanted poster, then he gave each of his hands the picture after roundup as a present."

"I asked him if he worked for the undertaker," Slocum said. "I understand what he meant now when he said sometimes." Pictures of the dead were often the only memory a family had of a small child who died or a patriarch who had lived far past the limits of mortal toil.

"Families are all he does since no outlaws ever come through here. There's nothing much to steal, except maybe for the cattle rustling."

"Is there a lot of that?" Slocum asked.

April shivered. Her lack of clothing wasn't the reason for her sudden chill.

"They get caught and hung fast in these parts. That makes life a whole lot easier for Marshal Dunbar. All he has to do is sit on his fat ass and pay court to that hussy in the café."

Slocum said nothing but considered this new tidbit. If Dunbar found out about him and Sara Beth Vincent, he would get tossed in the lockup so fast his head would spin. He wondered if Sara Beth encouraged the lawman, or if something more than a beefsteak on a plate in front of him was only a fantasy on the marshal's part.

"Enough, enough," Severigne said, clapping her hands. "You will do as Monsieur Molinari instructs, April." Severigne pointed and two of the other girls hung up a sheet behind April for a background.

"Velvet would be better, but this will do," Molinari

mumbled as he worked to put plates into his camera and draw out metal slides. "Show us some leg. No, no, more of what the men come for. Yes, that's it," he said when April more lewdly exposed herself.

Slocum watched and helped, doing whatever Molinari told for more than two hours. Every girl working for Severigne had her picture taken many times, some almost chaste and others downright lewd. Slocum couldn't figure out what Molinari saw in each, why he chose some poses for one woman and something completely different for another, so he asked.

Inside the parlor was brightly lit, making the windows into mirrors, but Slocum thought he saw movement outside once. Before he could go to investigate, Molinari demanded that he help him with another setup, moving the tripod about for a different angle. After he'd finished, Slocum went to the window, peered out, but saw nothing in the night. He returned to the side of the room, watching and waiting for Molinari to finish.

Molinari shrugged as he put the last of his plates into a special carrying case.

"It's an artist's eye, that's all. Some of them look chaste, so I shoot them nasty. Others have the appearance of a slut, so I try to soften them and make them look like the girl next door. The idea is to entice by giving the viewer something that fights with his preconceived ideas."

"This will make a good scrapbook," Severigne said.

Molinari almost sneered when he said, "There will be no 'scrapbook.' This will be your catalog, your pictures for the discerning gentleman to choose from."

Slocum got the idea. Rather than parading the girls in front of every cowboy who came into the brothel, Severigne could show the pictures and let the customer choose that way. Why give them a free look when they could pay for the real thing?

"Help me get my equipment loaded," Molinari said to Slocum.

"Yes, yes, go with him if he wants you to help him at his studio in town. So, use him as you like, Andrew. He has a strong back," Severigne said. She looked hard at Slocum, defying him to argue. He didn't.

He carried the camera out this time, but Molinari refused to allow him to help with the slotted case holding the dozens of exposed photographic plates.

"I do not want to waste more time shooting them again," Molinari said with some distaste.

Slocum climbed up onto the hard seat alongside Molinari, barely bracing himself before the photographer snapped the reins and got the team moving back to town.

"You in town much?" Slocum asked. "I've been here a few days but haven't seen you around."

"I spend a couple weeks a month touring the area. I make more than enough off these trips to live on, but small jobs like the one tonight furnish me with . . . luxuries."

Molinari spoke grandly, as if this were a trip to see the crowned heads of Europe.

"Luxuries? You mean Severigne will let you have any of her girls?"

"No!" Molinari moved away from Slocum as if he had come down with the plague. "I would never sleep with any of them. I do not want to catch a disease. I refer to the finer things. A good wine, oysters, food you cannot usually find in a godforsaken hole like Clabber Crossing."

"So you've done photographs like this before? You seemed to know what you wanted."

"I know what look in the women that men seek," Molinari said. "I made a great deal of money during the war selling such pictures to the troops." He looked down his nose at Slocum. "To the Union troops. I would never sell such artwork to a rebel."

Slocum was more curious than offended.

"How much would a picture sell for? To a soldier?"

"Ten dollars was my going rate. If I had a truly fine model, twenty dollars was not out of the question."

Slocum let out a low whistle. That was a princely sum for a blue photograph. He wondered if Molinari would keep any prints for himself to sell. There were army forts peppered all over Wyoming and the men there would as likely appreciate a picture of a half-naked April as any soldier during the war. It got lonely out on the frontier.

"Yes," Molinari said, "I am sure this seems like a huge sum to pay, but my work is excellent. Taking the photograph is only the first step. Developing the plates and printing them require as much, if not more, skill. A speck of dust in the wrong place will make a photograph unacceptable. If a splotch of my special developing acid lingers overlong on a plate, it will ruin an otherwise perfect shot. There is considerable art necessary to go along with the science of chemistry and physics involved in taking photographs."

Molinari pulled back hard on the reins and brought the buckboard to a halt at the edge of town. Slocum had seen the building standing off by itself but had paid it no attention since it had seemed deserted.

"You need a sign advertising your business," he said.

Molinari snorted in contempt.

"Those who can afford my work know I am here. Why bother drawing the riffraff who might want to gawk but not buy?"

"Why, indeed," Slocum said dryly. Molinari paid no attention to the sarcasm.

"Get the equipment unloaded and place it in the rack inside to the right of the door. To the right now, nowhere else." Molinari scooted the carrying case for the exposed plates out of the rear of the wagon and carried them as if he had an armload of nitroglycerin ready to explode. He set the case down, opened his office door, then moved the photographic plates inside. Slocum waited for him to put them wherever he intended before swinging through the door with the long-legged tripod and other equipment.

He saw the rack right away and carefully placed the

equipment in it. While Molinari fussed with his precious plates, Slocum looked around the small room. Dozens of portraits hung on the walls. He recognized Clyde Clabber right away. On the opposite wall, as if this defined their relationship, he saw Martin Bray's photograph—an engraved brass plate readable from across the room attested to the banker's name. Both men had been posed identically with the same background. He found the combination revealing and wondered if Molinari had done it on purpose.

"You said you'd shot other women like you did Severigne's girls tonight. You got a book of them I could look at?"

"No." Molinari spoke coldly. His tone brooked no argument.

"You must have files around, and I won't—"

"Leave. I have no more use for you."

Slocum took that to mean several things, and he felt the same way about the photographer. He stepped out into the chilly night and looked down the dark road leading back to Severigne's. There was nothing more for him to do there tonight. The photographic album had been shot and the ladies were probably enjoying a night without a never-ending stream of men pouring into the house like ants at a picnic.

A smile came to his lips. He knew the restaurant would be closed at this time of night but maybe there was the chance of a late-night snack. Slocum went to see if Sara Beth might be able to help him with that hunger.

8

Slocum heard Severigne laughing. He moved through the kitchen and looked out into the dining room, where she sat with her coffee cup in both hands, leaning forward to listen to April. The conversation proceeded too low for him to overhear, but the madam found it greatly amusing. He went back to grab himself some food. He and Sara Beth had spent the night in the most delightful fashion and he had not returned to the brothel until almost four in the morning. With sunrise before six, he hadn't been able to get much sleep and needed the coffee to wake up.

He had worked herds for long hours in his day and knew the tricks to staying awake. With a herd of cattle, a moment's inattention could mean a stampede and men dying. Staying alert while working as a bouncer in a whorehouse wasn't going to be as difficult.

"Slocum!" Severigne called out. He put down his coffee cup and went to the dining room.

"You have heard what April has to say?"

"Can't say I did, but it wasn't from lack of trying," Slocum said.

Severigne laughed and said, "This is what I like about you, Slocum. You are honest."

"I reckoned you saw me, so there wasn't any point denying what I was doing."

"Men lie. It is their nature. But you are more clever. You tell the truth and hope that we believe it is a lie. When you then lie, we will think it is the truth. Clever, clever. But this is not listening to all April has to tell. Once more, my dear, once more tell what you have heard in town."

"From town, not in town," April said. "I heard it from a bank teller." She grinned widely. "Martin Bray is sure somebody has been stealing from him. He's making life miserable for all his employees, but none of them will fess up to it."

"He and the marshal are in bed together," Slocum said.

"This is so? I had not heard," Severigne said.

"No, no, John means they're in cahoots. Everyone thinks that, but Bray is afraid to go to the marshal because he thinks he might be involved."

"This is rich," she said. "The banker's pet lawman is helping someone steal from him."

"It gets better," April said. She looked straight at Slocum and said, "He wants you to work for him."

Slocum was a few hours short on sleep and wasn't sure he heard her right. He asked her to repeat what she'd just said, and he heard it the same way.

"I don't get that. You're saying Bray wants *me* to find who's stealing him blind?"

"That's what the teller overheard. Bray and his lawyer were arguing, and Bray thought you'd be perfect since everybody in town knows you don't cotton much to the marshal—and he doesn't like you."

"This would mean you and the marshal are not partners," Severigne said.

Slocum laughed at this and shook his head. He'd sooner see the marshal in hell than be considered his partner. The longer he stayed in Clabber Crossing, the crazier it got. If

Dunbar got wind of Slocum spending time with Sara Beth, that would probably win him another night in jail since she said Dunbar was sweet on her. If Marshal Dunbar thought Bray had hired him to stop embezzling at the bank—and that the banker thought the marshal was part of it—that would warrant a bullet in the back.

"I'm not getting mixed up in this," Slocum said. "If one doesn't gun me down, the other will."

"You work for me, Slocum," Severigne said, "and you will do this thing for Bray." She duplicated her donkey sound, then laughed uproariously.

"You're joking," Slocum said, but he had the gut feeling she wasn't. "What do you expect to get out of siccing me on Bray?"

"Information. I want to know every little secret Bray is hiding. I would use this against him. He denies me a loan! I will ruin him!"

"You and Clabber? Did Clabber tell you to do this?"

"Clabber is not to know. Keep this between you and me. Between us," Severigne said, looking hard at April. The other woman tried to look innocent and failed. April hadn't been innocent in ten years.

"What's it worth to you?" Slocum asked. "This could be dangerous."

"You are no stranger to this danger," Severigne said. A tiny smile danced on her lips. "You owe me two months."

"Six weeks," Slocum said. "I've already put in two weeks."

"I will give you back the month for bail money," Severigne said. "Wait! No argument. Accept it or not."

Slocum knew it was loco but something appealed to him about this, and he wasn't going to pass up the chance to win back four weeks of his servitude.

"Done."

"You will not slack off your work here. This is in addition," Severigne said. "The town will be readying for the rodeo, and so must we."

"That's why you wanted the catalog of the girls," Slocum said. Things fell into place now. Severigne wanted to streamline the process of moving men through her house when the cowboys all crowded into town in a couple of weeks.

"You do not concern yourself with my business or that of this house."

"Might be I'd have to poke around the bank after hours," he said, thinking that Sara Beth need not be lonely on those nights. "Scouting for a trail can't be predicted, and there's no telling where it might take me."

Severigne looked hard at him, then agreed. From her suspicious expression, she knew Slocum had some action going on in town that had nothing to do with either the bank or the marshal. Finding Bray's secrets and using them against him appealed more to her than getting the most work possible out of Slocum.

For a man just come to town, Slocum found himself being mighty popular.

"Do you deposit your receipts in the bank?" Slocum asked. Severigne's outraged look was all the answer he needed. He remembered that she had said Anna's belongings were stored in the bank, so it figured that every penny generated by the brothel was also on deposit in Bray's bank for safekeeping. She might think he was a jackass but he provided the only banking service to be had in town. "I'll need a reason to stop by the bank, then. Something that doesn't seem out of the ordinary."

"Take this to the teller," April said, hastily scribbling a note. "The cute one." When Slocum just stared at her, she added, "The one with all his hair. He's the only one working for Bray who isn't bald."

"Should I know what's in the note?" Slocum held it up. Both April and Severigne looked shocked.

"You would not read this note?" Severigne asked. She threw up her hands. "What am I to do with an honest man?"

"I know of a lot of things I'd like to do," April said. She winked at Slocum, bumped hips as she left, then called out to Severigne about getting fresh linens before the men showed up that night.

Slocum opened the note and quickly scanned it. All it said was, "Tonight after closing." He didn't need to know more than this. April was seeing the teller off the clock and not charging him for her charms.

He finished what chores he had and set off for town, approaching the bank with some caution. After their run-ins before, he wasn't certain Bray wouldn't open fire the instant he stepped into the bank, claiming he thought a robbery was occurring. April hadn't shown herself to be unreliable but Slocum had to consider her profession. Seeing the way she and Severigne were constantly maneuvering for information, for some gain, made him wary about getting involved.

Slocum wasn't inclined to beat around the bush. He opened the bank door and stepped inside to the cool, close lobby. Dark wood paneling on three walls made the interior into a cave. The tellers' cages stretched directly in front of him, with a desk off to the left where Martin Bray pored over a stack of books with a pen in hand. He squinted hard and didn't notice Slocum as he stepped up to the middle teller's cage.

"You're the only one with hair," Slocum said, startling the young man.

"I—" The teller looked to the men on either side of him and nodded. "You want to open an account because I have all my hair?"

"I don't care if the Arapaho scalp you, but April likes your hair." He passed over the note. The teller blushed a beet red when he read it. "You got an answer?"

"What is this? This isn't the Western Union office. No fraternizing," Bray called from his desk.

"Tell her yes," the teller said in a hoarse whisper. He dropped his eyes to the stack of money he had been counting, pretending to be hard at work on bank business. Slocum saw that he simply riffled through the money, his mind somewhere else.

It didn't take much to guess where that might be. After closing.

"Bray, I got every right to be in here. I was just—"

"Slocum, get your ass over here. Now!" The bank president stood and pointed to a chair across the desk from him.

"Go to hell." Slocum wanted to see if April's information was right. As he started for the door, Bray let out a choked sound behind him.

"I want to have a word with you."

Slocum turned slowly and saw how Bray looked as if he was going to pass a stone. The only reason he wouldn't have come across the lobby and slammed the door behind Slocum was that April had heard correctly.

"Sit down," Bray said gruffly, but the look in his eyes bordered on panic.

"I'm not opening an account in your bank," Slocum said loud enough for the tellers to overhear. "And maybe I should tell Severigne to close hers. A mason jar buried in the backyard is a damned sight friendlier."

"I, uh, yes." Bray cleared his throat and dismissed the two nearest tellers, ordering them to lunch in spite of it being hours before a reasonable mealtime. In a low voice Bray said, "I find myself in a terrible situation, Slocum. I want to pay you to help me out of it."

"You want to *hire* me? There's not enough tea in China for that."

"One hundred dollars." Slocum stood. "Five hundred. All right, five hundred!"

This was enough money to take the starch out of Slocum's legs. He dropped back into the chair, amazed that the banker would offer a man he hated such a princely sum. That more than anything else told of the extent of the embezzlement. Bray must be losing his starched shirt to the unknown thief to ever think of paying that much.

"I'm not a gun for hire," Slocum said.

"I don't want anyone killed. You're a clever man," Bray said grudgingly. "I can see that by the way you talk to the marshal. I want you to find who's stealing from me."

"How many men you got working here?"

"Those three. That's it."

"How'd they ever get their hand into your till? You count their box at the end of every day, don't you?"

"Of course I do. I just don't know how they're stealing."

"You think they might be breaking into your bank vault?" The idea came to Slocum how this would get him a whale of a lot more money than taking Bray's five hundred dollars. However much was stashed in the vault had to be many times that. He had robbed a bank or two in his day and would relish the prospect of emptying Bray's until there wasn't dust left for the termites.

"I've changed the combination several times. That didn't stop the thieving. I've gone over the books and it's slick, whatever they're doing. Did I say 'they'? Might be they're all in cahoots." Bray's arrogance was replaced with outright fear now.

"What's your boy do around here? He dresses mighty fine. You have him listed as an officer of the bank?"

"Randall is . . . something of a ne'er-do-well. He's the apple of his mother's eye."

"What about your missus? She work here, too?"

"No, nothing of the sort. Philomena tends our house and does charitable work around town."

"She on the church committee with the new preacher man?"

"What's Henry Dawson got to do with this? The thievery must have started months and months ago, maybe a year for it to be so widespread. That was long before the reverend came to town."

"Shame about his wife."

"That's your concern. I'm paying you good money to stop the theft from this bank. You—you're the only one I know who can't be involved since you just came to town." Something of Bray's obnoxious personality shone through his fear of losing even a dime. That notion caused Slocum to ask a question that had gone begging for an answer.

"How much?"

"I told you. Five hundred—and—" Bray clamped his mouth shut and rocked back in his chair. His jaw muscles tensed when he realized what Slocum was asking. "The bank has lost almost ten thousand dollars."

Slocum kept his best poker face on. He had expected the sum to be immense but had no idea it was so large. Banks had to keep a large reserve as guarantee against the loans outstanding. If anything happened that required Bray to cough up a large sum of money, he might not be able to do it. Thoughts of ransacking his vault fled. There might not be anything left to steal.

"You keep the marshal off my back, and I'll see what I can find. Unless there's something obvious like a tunnel into your vault, I'll have to ask a lot of questions and see whose answers don't fit. Most folks don't like answering, so I'll likely ruffle some feathers."

"Marshal Dunbar will not be a problem."

Slocum almost asked about Dunbar and Bray's partnership. Being the lawman in a town like Clabber Crossing afforded Dunbar the chance to steal. Who was there to watch the marshal? This was a peaceable community and not prone to crime.

"How many women've died in the past year or so?"

"What's that got to do with my problem?" Bray looked ready to chew nails and spit tacks when his two tellers returned.

"Back, sir. Done took our break and ready to work."

"You'll put in overtime tonight," Bray snapped. "Slackers."

"But you said we—" April's beau was the one who complained. Slocum wondered if he might also be brave enough to steal from the bank to impress the lovely Cyprian. Bray didn't seem the sort to be overly generous with his pay and keeping a woman like April in clover could be an expensive chore. Pleasurable, probably, but very expensive.

"So don't give me the loan," Slocum said loudly. He locked eyes with Bray, who nodded once at this diversion to explain why Slocum had been so long in the bank. "I'll get the money elsewhere."

"Get a job with a rancher, not a whoremonger like Severigne," Bray said. "And maybe this bank can see fit to give you that loan."

Slocum winked at April's boyfriend as he left, stepping into the hot sun. He had not realized how oppressive the interior of the bank was until the fresh breeze and burning sunlight surrounded him.

Although Bray had denied the possibility, Slocum circled the building, studying the ground for any sign that someone had tunneled into the vault. Even the best excavation would cause sagging in the ground over the tunnel unless they had dug down much deeper than common sense would dictate. On his second trip around the bank, finding nothing, he looked up to see a boy running away. It wasn't the marshal's courier, Jed, though he was close in age. This one had dark hair that reminded him of Emily Dawson.

Slocum scratched his head, wondering if the Peeping Tom he had almost seen several times was none other than the preacher's son. It was one more Clabber Crossing mystery that would eventually come to light. Right now, he had to see if Sara Beth might want to take a break just before the noontime crowd elbowed their way into her restaurant. After that, she might even give him some of the information he needed to solve Martin Bray's theft problem.

But Slocum wasn't going to rush getting to that. No, sir.

9

"The whole town's going to starve if I keep closing the restaurant in the middle of the day," Sara Beth said, snuggling closer to Slocum in the tiny bed. The heat of her body was fine, but the late morning sunlight slanted through the curtained window and turned the room into a furnace. As hot as it had been between the two of them a little while before, it was even hotter now. Uncomfortably so.

Slocum turned so he could sprawl on his back. Sara Beth moved to put her head on his chest.

"You've got such a strong heart," she said.

Slocum kept looking toward the window and thought he saw a shadow pass by outside. It might have been his imagination, but he had come to doubt it.

"What do you know of Edgar Dawson?"

"That's a strange question to ask," she said. The blonde moved to lie alongside him so only their hips touched. Sweat began turning their skin slippery and quickly even this bit of intimacy became too much for them. They slid even farther apart, but Sara Beth kept her hand on Slocum's belly, as if her fingers might slip down a bit lower and try to resurrect the momentarily dead.

"I think he's been spying on purty near everyone in town, but you especially."

"Me? Why, Emily and I were friends. I was over at their house many times and he was always polite." She fell silent. Slocum felt her hand tense as she dug fingernails into his stomach. "Now that you mention it, he was a bit too attentive. I never saw a boy want to fetch for his momma's friends like he did."

"You're a mighty fine-looking woman, and you could lead the men in this town around by their noses. You said Dunbar was always coming along after you. Why not the preacher's son, too?"

"I've got what I want," she said. Her hot breath gusted across his bare chest. At another time, a cooler time, that would have been exciting. Now it only added to Slocum's feeling he was being boiled alive.

"You and Emily were friends. What about her and the banker's wife?"

"Philomena? Oh, I saw her there often enough at the church. She did a considerable amount of sociable work, but she always avoided me like I had leprosy. A working woman wasn't of the same cultural class, you know."

"Who else would be in Clabber Crossing?"

"Nobody, and Philomena Bray let everyone know it, too. She came from some filthy rich Boston family. Heaven knows why she married Martin."

"He's a banker," Slocum pointed out. "She might think being a big fish in a small pond like Clabber Crossing was better than swimming around with the really well-off back in Boston."

"Could be. Seems like she exiled herself here, though."

"Almost as if she wanted to get as far away as possible," Slocum said, thinking aloud. "Do you know for a fact that she came from a rich family?"

"That's what everyone says," Sara Beth answered. "It really doesn't matter so much, does it? She's here, she's rich, and she lets everyone know it at the drop of a hat. All she ever wanted from her charity was to be known for it. Who she helped—if anyone—didn't matter as much as everyone thanking her for being so caring."

"That must have rankled Henry Dawson. He struck me as a man of deep convictions."

"Just like Emily. Deeply devoted to doing God's work."

"You still on good terms with the preacher?"

"I suppose, though I was certainly better friends with Emily. After all, Henry *is* the pastor. I can't imagine getting too friendly with him, if you know what I mean."

"Why don't you go talk to him about Philomena? I'd like to listen in."

"It'll cost you," Sara Beth said. She moved her hand and squeezed down with enough force to make Slocum grumble. "Oh, very well. Not now, but later."

"Make it a rain check," Slocum said.

"Oh, my, aren't you the romantic one wanting to make love in the rain?"

That hadn't been on his mind at all. As he got dressed, he was thinking hard about all the possible reasons Emily might have killed herself—or gotten herself killed. She might have talked with Philomena and learned something about the embezzlement from the bank. Martin Bray wasn't the kind to believe his wife—or any woman—had a lick of sense, but Philomena might have mentioned something to Emily about the embezzlement that got the woman killed.

Slocum tried to picture any of the three tellers murdering Emily Dawson and couldn't do it, but what did a killer look like? A man who might have a scheme to steal thousands of dollars without getting caught would do most anything if he was going to be exposed. It would hurt both his pride and his poke. Still, those tellers all looked the sort to spook easily. They'd hightail it out of town rather than commit murder.

But that didn't leave a whole passel of folks who might be dipping into the bank's vault. Bray had mentioned having a lawyer. Slocum didn't trust lawyers as far as he could throw them. He mentally corrected that. Nowhere near as far because he'd be inclined to throw them over a tall cliff. Who better to insinuate himself into the bank's accounts than a crooked lawyer?

If the lawyer and Philomena were in cahoots, that made the crime all the easier. Bray looked like a pinchpenny and a woman used to traveling in high society circles back in Boston might consider salting some money away before leaving him.

Slocum heaved a deep sigh when he realized he might as well have been smoking loco weed for all the truth in any of it. He needed something more definite before spinning wild tales—and with the facts, they'd be the truth, not stories to tell around a campfire.

"I don't know, John. This doesn't seem right. I don't mind talking to the pastor, but his wife's just died and you eavesdropping and all. It's just not right."

"No, it isn't," Slocum said, giving Sara Beth a quick kiss. "But you'll do it anyway."

"For you." Her lips thinned to a line. "No, for Emily. You're going to find out what happened to her."

Slocum felt beholden to a lot of people in Clabber Crossing—and they were all women. He wondered how he had gotten himself into such a pickle.

They left the back of the restaurant and took separate paths to the church. Slocum watched carefully to see if anyone noticed them leaving Sara Beth's or heading in the same general direction. The town was still sluggish from the growing heat, although a strong breeze had kicked up and brought some promise of cooler weather from the far distant Grand Tetons. Slocum looped around and went to the abandoned cabin where Emily Dawson had asked to meet. Her body was gone and nothing he found poking around in the debris in the main room gave him evidence one way or the other. She might have killed herself, but why would she bother passing him the note so secretly? The woman had something she wanted to tell him.

But why him?

It was a puzzlement.

Slocum quit hunting for what wasn't here and made his way up the hill to the church. The small house behind it was the likeliest spot for Sara Beth to meet with the preacher, so he headed there. The windows were open and the lace curtains snapped fitfully in the rising wind, but their sound didn't muffle the conversation going on inside.

"It's good of you to come by, Miss Vincent," the preacher said. "Emily often spoke of you and how good a friend you were to her."

"I'm so sorry about what happened, Reverend Dawson," Sara Beth said. Slocum looked inside and saw her facing the window. She made a shooing motion with her hand to warn him to hide himself better.

"Is there a fly annoying you?" Henry Dawson asked. "I should get more fly strips, but then there are so many things I should do. Somehow, I haven't had the gumption to just *do* them."

Slocum settled down to listen without being seen, but the conversation rambled, touched on things he had no interest in. He was almost at the point of popping back up in the window to signal to Sara Beth to get down to the point when he saw a boy poke his head around the corner of the house and stare at him, unblinking.

Not knowing what to do, Slocum simply stared back until the boy vanished. Slocum started to go after him because he was sure this was Edgar Dawson and the boy would tell his pa, but Sara Beth finally asked a question Slocum wanted answered.

"This isn't proper for me to mention, but I happened to overhear Philomena tell Emily about money problems. I thought it was odd she was asking my wife rather than coming to me, but sometimes folks are more comfortable with their own kind."

"Emily was easy to talk to," Sara Beth said. "What kind of money problems? Sometimes I don't have enough money to buy the best steaks for the restaurant, but I usually have enough for eggs. That kind of problem?"

"I think it was more serious," Reverend Dawson said.

"But Philomena is the banker's wife. I can't imagine Mr. Bray letting his wife do without."

"Martin is a frugal man."

Sara Beth laughed, just a tinge of bitterness in it, then said, "'Frugal' wasn't the word I had in mind. Mr. Bray is an outright skinflint."

"I won't argue that," Dawson said, chuckling.

"If there is anything I can do for you, please let me know. It's not easy losing a spouse."

"Yes, you would know. You lost your husband, didn't you?"

"I did," Sara Beth said brusquely. "Now I really must go. The town needs to be fed, and I'm the best one to do it."

"I'll stop by for coffee and some pie," Dawson said.

"You order what you want, Reverend, and it will be on the house. I know your money situation is tight."

"The repairs to the church cost so much," Henry Dawson said almost wistfully.

Sara Beth bade him good-bye, and Slocum joined her on the road back into town. She bounced along, and he found it difficult to concentrate because of the motion.

"I'm so happy, John! I found out what you wanted to know. Philomena Bray was in financial straits."

"Why? Why couldn't she go to her husband?" Slocum's mind raced with this new tidbit of gossip. He had thought Philomena might have been embezzling from the bank, but Bray said the theft had gone on for some time and Philomena had told Emily how she needed money. If as much had been stolen from the bank as Bray said, his wife would be rolling in clover. There was nowhere in a town the size of Clabber Crossing to spend wildly. With Bray owning the only bank in town, it behooved him to be sure his wife was well dressed and possessed of the finer things so he could lord it over Clyde Clabber and anyone calling the town's namesake friend.

"I wouldn't ask Bray for the time of day. Knowing him, he'd charge me for it."

"You've got to talk to Philomena. You know her, don't you?"

"Not that well. We certainly don't travel in the same social circle."

"How many social circles can there be in a place like this?" Slocum asked.

Sara Beth laughed and again it carried a bitterness to it that surprised him.

"More than you think. No one talks to Severigne or her girls, no one decent, but nobody talks to Philomena either, because she's at the top of the social strata."

"What about you?"

"I . . . I don't mind being under you, socially speaking," Sara Beth said, giving him a wicked smile. "Mostly, I find myself something of an outcast since my husband died. The married women won't have anything to do with me, and the unmarried ones are all fifteen years old. Or so it seems. Come this time next year, they'll be married, too."

"Do you think Philomena confided in Emily because they knew each other?"

"Of course they did. Philomena worked for the church to raise money." Sara Beth eyed him harder. "You meant something else, don't you? I don't see how they could have known each other. Philomena married Bray years ago, somewhere back East."

"You know where?"

"I don't remember hearing."

"Ask her that, too."

"John, I have to—" She saw how determined he was. "Oh, very well. But you'll owe me."

"I always pay my debts, especially to the prettiest lady in all of Wyoming."

"Only Wyoming? Not west of the Mississippi?"

"Quit fishing for compliments. You know you're pretty."

"A girl likes to hear it from her beau."

For an instant Slocum thought Sara Beth was going to kiss him in public, but she turned and headed for a road leading away from town. On the top of a low hill stood a large house that must belong to the banker. Slocum let Sara Beth go, as he had before, circled, and came up on the house from the rear. Bray was at the bank so he didn't have any worry about being seen—or so he thought until he heard gravel crunch behind him.

He half turned but something hard and heavy crashed into the side of his head, knocking him to the ground. Stunned, he lay there. Through pain-misted eyes he saw a boot kicking straight for his belly. He curled up in a tight ball and brought his arms around in time to rob the blow of much of its power.

It still scooted him along the ground and made his forearms hurt like fire. Before his attacker could wind up for another kick, Slocum forced himself outward, got his hands and knees under him, then pushed to his feet. He swung around and caught a hard fist to the belly that almost knocked the wind from him. Doubling over, he grabbed and caught a second fist coming to add to the damage of the first. He clung to the arm with all his strength, then spun enough to drive his shoulder into his attacker's chest, knocking him back.

Slocum let go and stumbled back. He grabbed for his six-shooter and drew.

He had Randall Bray dead in his sights.

"Don't go for it. You'll be dead before you clear leather," Slocum warned.

Bray ignored him and grabbed for the pistol at his hip.

10

Slocum was still off-balance when he fired. The recoil threw him sideways and this kept Randall Bray's bullet from cutting through his chest. Slocum dropped to one knee, ready to get off a second shot, but Bray had already tried to fire. His gun jammed.

"You're a dead man if you don't drop it. You'll never get off another shot before I kill you." Slocum made a point of cocking his Colt Navy and pointing it directly at Bray's face. For the young gunman it had to look as if he stared into the mouth of hell itself.

"You're gonna die. I'm gonna fix you and that evil bitch good." Bray threw his pistol at Slocum, who dodged it easily. By the time Slocum recovered, Bray was running off across the field directly behind the house, heading for a wooded area some distance off. Slocum could have sent a few rounds winging after him to keep him going but decided not to waste the ammunition.

He shoved his six-shooter back into his holster and picked up Bray's gun. The hammer was caught halfway back, making it impossible to fire. Slocum saw that little care had been expended on the pistol. His own Colt was like a watch, a fine precision instrument that required constant care. Seldom a day went by that Slocum didn't take it apart, oil parts that needed oiling, and clean parts that had accumulated a film of trail dust. When he had to rely on getting off an accurate first shot, a few minutes spent on daily maintenance were a small price to pay.

It had saved his life today.

He looked toward the house and saw Sara Beth coming out. She took Philomena Bray's hands in her own, then bent over and touched cheeks with the woman before hurrying off. Slocum made sure that Randall Bray was nowhere to be seen, then worked his way around to meet up with Sara Beth on the road leading back to Clabber Crossing.

"Was she upset?" Slocum asked.

"About what?"

"The gunshots."

"Oh, she said her son does target practice all the time. She wasn't the least worried about that, but she did show a considerable upset when I asked about where she and Martin got married."

"It wasn't back East," Slocum said.

"Well, it was, but not too far east. They met and after a whirlwind romance married in Kansas City. She said she has no idea how the notion she comes from Boston society got started."

"Did she know Emily there?"

"She wouldn't say but I got the feeling that they might have met earlier than Emily's coming to Clabber Crossing. Perhaps they were acquaintances rather than friends?"

"Maybe," Slocum said. "Did you find anything about her money troubles?"

"That's why I left. She became very distant, as if she wanted to be somewhere else—anywhere else. Philomena certainly did not wish to discuss with me what she had with Emily, yet I offered some assistance."

"What did you offer her?" Slocum asked, surprised.

"I thought it might be interesting to watch her reaction if

I suggested a loan of a few dollars. Well, a few hundred. Not that I have it, but she can't know that since the restaurant is always busy. Which reminds me, I need to get back to the kitchen and finish the fixings for this evening's meal. You'd be surprised how many cowboys come in off the trail famished."

"For food, too," Slocum said. "Mostly, I suspect they just want to ogle you."

"Like you do?"

"I hope not," Slocum said. "Some ogling is best left private."

"You are so much fun, John." Sara Beth stood on tiptoe and gave him a quick kiss before rushing back to the restaurant. Slocum followed discreetly and watched her duck into the small building. Before he had crossed to the far end of town, smoke billowed from the chimney pipe in her kitchen.

He pushed thoughts of the lovely blonde from his head as he made his way back to Severigne's house. Getting Martin Bray to hire him had been easy enough, but little he had found out had any bearing on the man's problem. Or did it?

Something about Emily's death and her friendship with Philomena bothered him. The banker's wife couldn't be stealing since she needed more money and possibly had asked Emily Dawson for it. Yet she wouldn't take a dime from Sara Beth when a loan was offered. That made him wonder if Philomena and Emily had known each other better than they had let on before they had arrived in Clabber Crossing. Philomena had been here for a couple years, Emily for a few months.

"Kansas City," he mused. "That might have been where their paths crossed, but why didn't Henry Dawson make mention of that?"

The only reason Slocum could come up with was that Emily and Philomena wanted their Kansas City friendship kept a secret. But why?

He took the back steps into Severigne's kitchen two at a

time. Somehow he wasn't surprised to see her waiting for him, but he was startled when he saw that she had been crying.

"What's wrong?" he asked.

"They have been taken away. Kidnapped!"

"Who?"

"Danielle and Catherine. I let them sleep late this morning, almost to ten, then went to their room. Both were gone! Missing!"

"How do you know they were kidnapped?"

"Alice saw them last night with two men. Very late, but she thought nothing of it."

"Did you get a ransom note?"

"No, none. I am so distraught. Such a thing has never happened to me before. Not here. Before, the girls were taken and killed after being foully used by Parisian cutthroats. But out here in the West I did not expect such crude behavior. Drunkenness, yes. Even some slapping around, but not this. They are such good girls!"

"I want to talk to Alice."

"She is in the parlor. I will go with you and—"

"No." Slocum was curt enough that Severigne rocked back.

"They are my responsibility. They are my girls!"

"Did you let the marshal know?"

"Dunbar? No!"

"I can guess the reason. You don't think he could track them down. So let me work however I have to."

Severigne only nodded. Her lips quivered, and she might not trust herself to speak further without crying. The madam's emotions were real, and she was upset over the missing women, but Slocum wondered exactly how "kidnapped" they were.

Alice looked up when he came into the parlor, then hastily turned so she stared out the window toward an open field.

"Who were they?"

"I'da thought Severigne would have told you. Catherine and Danielle. They—"

"She told me that. Who were the men they left with?"

"They must have been kidnapped. They—"

"They went willingly. Their rooms . . ." He let the sentence trail off.

"I told them to leave their belongings, but they couldn't do that. They had to take their clothes with them." Alice turned back and stared at Slocum. "Don't fetch them back. They found themselves men who want to marry them."

"Just like that? The men come in for a tumble and the two whores believe they want to marry them?"

"It could happen."

Slocum snorted in contempt at such an idea. The two women might have ridden off willingly, but he doubted the men wanted to marry them. More likely they would rape them and leave a pair of bodies for the buzzards out on the prairie. For all of Severigne's protests that this couldn't happen out here where a man's word was his bond, Slocum had known more than one man with no morals at all. Cowboys might be polite enough, but some were just plain mean and some were worse—they enjoyed raping and killing.

"You know what spread the cowboys worked?" Alice shook her head. "You have any idea where they'd head?"

"Danielle said they were going west, into the mountains. One of 'em is supposed to have a cabin there."

"You don't say a word of any of this to Severigne," Slocum said. "She's upset enough thinking two of her girls were kidnapped. No telling what she'd do if she heard they'd gone on their own to get away from her."

"It wasn't like that, John," protested Alice. "All of us, we all want to find a guy to marry. Most of the men who come to see us are drunks or worse. These two had money and treated Catherine and Danielle real good."

"Not a word to Severigne," he said sternly. Alice nodded. From her reaction he wondered if she felt a touch of envy—or was it sadness that the men hadn't picked her?

Slocum went to the kitchen, where Severigne sat, composing herself. If he hadn't known she had been crying, he would never have guessed, except for the redness in her eyes.

"I can track them down. They don't have more than a half-day's start and traveling with your two girls will slow them down."

"What do they want? I will pay. For the sake of Danielle and Catherine, I will pay anything." Severigne settled down and amended, "Almost anything."

"I'll need supplies and another horse to make the best time."

Severigne waved her hand, giving him anything he wanted. Slocum left without another word, fetched his horse, and then chose another to use as a pack animal. He wouldn't take much in the way of supplies but intended to switch from one horse to the next. He could travel fifty miles in a day that way—more, if necessary. Supplies were needed so he wouldn't have to stop and forage. Living in the saddle wasn't anything he looked forward to, but he had a feeling in his gut that the men who had sweet-talked Catherine and Danielle weren't likely to be as sweet when they got to the cabin in the mountains or wherever they were taking the women.

Slocum rode into town, got his supplies from Aronson at the general store, and started on the trail westward. He hadn't ridden a mile when he got the feeling of being watched. Craning around in the saddle, he watched his back trail for a few minutes before he spotted a cloud of dust in the road, moving toward him.

Thoughts of Randall Bray fixing his pistol came to mind, but Slocum was less afraid of the hothead than he was of losing time on the trail. He reckoned the men would stay on this road because of the women. Not only could they make better time, but the ladies weren't as likely to protest heading out across country. Slocum understood folks from towns. To them, traveling along a road meant they were heading somewhere. Lighting out where there wasn't a road made them uneasy, sure they were getting themselves lost.

The dust cloud came closer. Whoever kicked it up was in a powerful hurry. Slocum reached down and slid the leather thong off the hammer of his Colt. That loop kept the pistol from bouncing out as he rode. Now he might have to pull it fast.

"John, John! Thanks for finally waiting for me! You surely do ride fast."

Slocum pushed the keeper back over the six-gun's hammer and slumped a little in the saddle. He had expected trouble and what he got was even worse. He couldn't shoot his way out of this.

Sara Beth tugged hard on her horse's reins and brought it to a halt a few yards away.

"How dare you try to leave town and not even say goodbye to me!"

"I wasn't leaving. I've got a chore to do."

"Some chore, with a horse all weighed down with supplies so you don't have to stop until you're far away from me!"

"I'll be back as soon as I track them down."

"Them?"

Slocum found himself explaining to Sara Beth rather than just turning his back on her and riding along on the trail.

"So you're not running out on me?"

"Severigne thinks her two girls have been kidnapped, but there's more to it since no ransom notes were left. Unless I miss my guess, Danielle and Catherine have got themselves in a heap of trouble."

"You think the two cowboys will kill them?"

"If the women are lucky."

Sara Beth turned pale, then said, "Then let's get after

them. Right now! The longer you sit there jawing, the more likely that is to happen."

"Head on back to town. You'll only slow me down."

"Oh, think I can't keep up? I want to help. When you find them, they'll need someone to settle them right down, and I'm the one to do that."

"There's likely to be at least two dead before I finish," Slocum said grimly. He didn't cotton to woman-stealing, and that's the way he read this spoor. Bringing the men back for trial would be useless.

"That way? They took this road west?" Sara Beth didn't wait for his answer. She kicked at her horse's flanks and shot off like a rocket. Slocum considered hog-tieing her and leaving her behind but that would be too dangerous.

Would it be as dangerous for her if she rode with him? He didn't know but figured he could ride her into the ground.

He was wrong.

All night long they rode, Sara Beth never flagging. Her horse didn't carry as much weight as Slocum's, and even when he switched back and forth, he wasn't able to tucker out Sara Beth's horse. He felt a little wobbly in the saddle from lack of sleep, but when dawn crept over the horizon at their backs, Sara Beth didn't look any more tired than when she'd overtaken him outside town.

"There," Slocum said, drawing rein. He rubbed his tired eyes and got the sleep out of them, then hopped to the ground and studied the grass and cut-up dirt beside the road. "They lit out across country here." He made out tracks from four horses. While this might be another party, how many foursomes heading west right now were there? He hadn't sighted a single rider in either direction along the road. Wyoming was mighty big and mighty barren.

"The tracks lead up into the hills," Sara Beth said. "Even I can see that. But how did you spot them in the first place, John?"

He didn't bother answering. There were better trackers

out there, but there were a whole lot worse. The cowboys didn't even try to hide their hoofprints as they made for the high country.

"You think there's a cabin up ahead?"

"I don't see any smoke."

"Might not want to take the time to build a fire. They've been on the trail all night, and if I know cowboys, they're mighty horny right about now."

A scream cut through the still morning. Slocum turned, and when a second cry echoed down from the heights, he got a better sense of where the women had to be.

"Stay here," Slocum said. He tossed the reins of the second horse to Sara Beth, then put his heels to his horse, bounding up the hill. He didn't worry much about sneaking up on the cowboys. If anything, the more noise he made, the more likely they were to be distracted from what they intended doing with the women.

Slocum pounded ahead and burst through a wall of trees into a clearing. Two horses grazed fitfully at clumps of grass near where a cowboy was ripping off the clothes of a struggling woman. At this range Slocum couldn't identify the woman but knew she had to be one of those he sought.

He galloped forward, yelling at the top of his lungs. He caught flashes of everything happening. The woman was naked to the waist, her bodice ripped and hanging in shreds. Part of her skirt had been torn also, but she clung to it to prevent the cowboy from stripping her completely naked.

In one hand the man held a bottle of whiskey—an almost empty bottle. If he was responsible for draining that much, it was a surprise he could even stand, much less think about raping the woman.

"You git on away," the cowboy shouted. He tried to point the bottle at Slocum, then realized his error. Dropping the bottle, he pulled out his six-shooter and got off a couple rounds. Slocum kept on, intent on riding the man down. A few kicks from his horse's front hooves would solve the problem quickly.

But Slocum had too far to go and the cowboy wasn't drunk enough to be entirely stupid. He grabbed the woman and whirled her around. One arm held her firmly about the waist as he held his six-shooter dangerously close to her.

"You want her? You ain't gonna get her. Not 'til after I'm done."

Slocum slowed his headlong assault and pulled up a few yards away.

"You don't have any call to shoot her. Let Danielle go." He was finally close enough to recognize the woman, in spite of her face being scrunched up in fear. Dirt made her even harder to identify, but she didn't contradict him using her name.

"She's mine. I stole her fair 'n' square."

"Why'd you go and kidnap a whore? For two bits you could have had her and everyone would have been happy," Slocum said.

"Ain't my way to pay fer what I kin git fer free."

"Might be we can work something out," Slocum said. Danielle looked at him, her eyes wide in fear.

"He's crazy drunk. Don't say a thing like that! You don't know what he's been sayin' he intends to do to me!"

"Just this once," Slocum said, dismounting. As he slipped to the ground, he pulled the leather thong off the hammer of his Colt. "That wouldn't be so bad, now would it? He's a good-looking man. You can do him for free, Danielle. This one time, special-like."

"You git on outta here. I don't know you and I don't want to." The cowboy swung his six-gun around and pointed it at Slocum.

"We can settle this. I know we can, the three of us."

"Ain't no three of us. Jist me and the whore." The cowboy started to shoot but Danielle elbowed him in the ribs. Too much booze had deadened his sensations. He grunted but didn't loosen his grip on her—and then he did the very thing that Slocum feared most.

The cowboy cocked his six-shooter and put the gun to Danielle's temple.

"I'm gittin' tired of all this talk. I don't need her alive fer what I intend doin'."

Slocum was out of position to draw and fire. He would hit Danielle—but maybe that would be a boon for her. He started to draw, then froze when he saw how hard the cowboy had jammed the gun into the woman's temple.

"Say yer good-byes, bitch!"

11

"Why not have two of us?"

The cowboy blinked and then squinted. He half turned to see Sara Beth astride her horse. She lifted one leg, showing bare flesh all the way up to the thigh as she swung her leg over the saddle horn.

"I'll be—" the cowboy started. He never finished his sentence. Slocum drew, aimed, and fired in one smooth movement. The bullet hit the man in the side of the head, killing him instantly. As his gun fell from lifeless fingers, Danielle began screaming.

Sara Beth dropped from the horse and ran to the woman, taking her in her arms and cooing to her as if she were a small child. As she moved Danielle away, hiding the dead body from her crying, hysterical ward, she inclined her head toward the body. Slocum was already moving to put himself between Danielle and the cowboy's corpse on the ground. He kicked away the fallen six-shooter and dropped to one knee. He didn't have to check for a pulse. The sightless eyes told the story. His shot had blown away the far side of the cowboy's head when it exited.

Slocum went through the cowboy's pockets and pulled out a watch and a few dollars, folded up and tucked away.

"You robbing the dead?" Sara Beth asked acidly.

Slocum handed up the money and the watch.

"It's for her. She deserves something out of this. Does he have a name?"

"H-His partner called him Lew."

"I don't see anything to tell where he worked. It wouldn't be too good to let his boss know what he tried to do. No reason not to let him think his hand just drifted on and didn't bother telling him." Slocum stood. "You want to ride on back to town with her? I'll see to burying this piece of—"

"I can make it on my own. I don't want anyone with me. Nobody."

"Why not?" Sara Beth asked. "You ought to have somebody along for company."

"He sent you. He's after me. That's why I went with Lew. I wanted away, but I didn't know what he'd try to do."

"What are you talking about?" Slocum spoke to thin air. Danielle pushed Sara Beth away and ran for the horses still cropping grass. Without hardly slowing, she dragged herself into the saddle and raced off, going deeper into the woods and ignoring Sara Beth's call for her to stop.

"We have to get her, John. She's confused, crazy with fear."

"Let her go," he said. "She was running from something at Severigne's—or someone. You have any idea who it was?"

"He must have been terrible to make her think somebody like that was her salvation." Sara Beth looked as if she would spit on Lew's corpse. "But I don't know who it would be. You work there. Did she have troubles with anybody in particular?"

"Not that I saw, but Severigne handled all those kinds of problems unless the customer got belligerent. I haven't had to throw out but a couple drunks." He turned grim as a thought occurred to him that Randall Bray might be the one Danielle feared. Everything the banker's son did seemed aimed at hurting Severigne. After all, Slocum was sure Bray had tried to burn the house to the ground. If the fire hadn't been put out quickly, a half dozen of Severigne's Cyprians might have died in the flames.

"Who are you thinking of?" Sara Beth demanded. "Is it Randall Bray? I never liked that little sneak. He was always so nasty, like he was better than everybody else. And the things he's said to me!"

"Catherine's still out there," Slocum interrupted. He considered the time it would take to bury Lew deep enough to keep the coyotes from having a feast. Slocum had nothing against coyotes and didn't want them to get a bellyache dining on such tainted flesh, but the other woman was likely in as big a world of trouble as Danielle.

Time crushed down, and burying Lew would take a long time since Slocum didn't have a shovel. He thought of Aronson's stack of shovels and how the general store owner thought he had wanted one. Now that he did, the store was miles distant.

"That cabin you mentioned," Sara Beth said.

"Yeah?" Slocum looked in the direction the woman pointed. A tiny curl of white wood smoke rose above the trees. He reloaded his pistol and said, "Can't be more than a mile off. Less."

"You going to try to order me to stay?"

"Just don't go doing any damn fool thing like you just did. He could have killed Danielle and you."

"If I hadn't distracted him, you'd never have gotten a clean shot. You're good with that six-gun, aren't you?"

Slocum didn't answer. He stepped up into the saddle and turned his pony's face for the direction of the smoke. It wasn't even eight o'clock in the morning and he had already killed a man. What was the next hour to bring?

His nostrils expanded as he caught the smell of food cooking. Someone was frying bacon. His belly growled and reminded him how long it had been since eating anything but a strip of tough, salty jerky while riding along during the night.

"There, John. Through the trees." Sara Beth pointed out the cabin he had already seen.

"I suppose I ought to just ride up and shoot the son of a bitch," Slocum said, more to himself than to the woman. "That'd save a bunch of time and avoid more unpleasantness."

"Do it, John. I saw what that cowboy was trying to do to Danielle."

Slocum dismounted, drew his six-shooter, and walked up to the door. He took a deep breath, then kicked open the door, his pistol coming up. He released his touch on his trigger when he saw only Catherine sitting in a chair on the far side of a small table.

"Where is he?"

"John, what are you doing?" The woman put down a spoon so hard that it clattered on the table and she spilled some of the oatmeal she had been eating from a bowl.

"Severigne sent me to bring you back."

"I—" Catherine didn't get any farther. From behind him Slocum heard a roar of anger. He lowered his arm, spun, and started to draw a bead. The burly man bowled him over, his powerful arms circling around Slocum's shoulders like steel bands.

Slocum fired once, hoping to hit the man in the leg. His bullet dug a hole in the door and then he was flat on his back, the cowboy trying to smash his forehead into Slocum's face.

He fired again and felt the cowboy wince. This gave him all the opening he was likely to get. Slocum pulled his left hand free, struck hard on the side of the man's head, and dislodged him. He got his knees up, kicked hard, and shoved away from the cowboy so he could come to his knees and raise his six-shooter for a killing shot.

"No, John, no! You'll have to shoot me first!" Catherine slid in front of the stunned cowboy, who shook his head, regained his senses, and lifted her off her feet to put her behind him.

"You shoot me, not her!"

"Don't hurt him. Will's a good man. Don't hurt him." Once more Catherine moved with a sinuous grace and interposed herself between the cowboy and Slocum's pistol.

"You want to be with him?"

"I don't owe Severigne anything. She doesn't own me and I can leave whenever I want. You tell her that. You tell her I love Will Hudson and we're going to get married."

"You hush, Catherine," the cowboy said. "You don't owe him nothing. You don't have to explain nothing to him."

Slocum rocked back and got to his feet, the six-gun still pointed in the direction of the hulk of a man.

"Let me get this straight. You two are good together?" He saw from their expressions the truth. "What about Danielle and Lew?"

"I never heard his name other than Lew. He was a drifter I met up with at McCavity's Saloon. Me and Catherine was planning on running away for weeks. Him and Danielle just tagged along."

"You didn't know what he intended to do to her?" Their silence spoke louder than any denial. They didn't know because they had come here to the cabin. From the messy blanket on the bed, Slocum knew what had been on their minds. "Why not tell Severigne you were taking off?"

"I wanted to, but Catherine said Severigne would talk her out of it. She's got a silver tongue, that one. I don't speak too good sometimes, but I love her." Will put his arm around the woman's shoulders to protect her.

"You work for one of the ranchers?" Slocum asked.

"Will's foreman on the Flying B Ranch."

"You can ride on over the hill to the main house. Go past the bunkhouse to the trail past the barn and ask Mr. Bascomb. I've worked for him five seasons now."

Slocum slid his six-shooter back into its holster.

"I'll tell Severigne. If you send her an invitation to the wedding, that'd go a long way toward smoothing her ruffled feathers."

"I, uh, I'm not sure. You see, Mr. Bascomb and his wife don't know what I was doin' back at Clabber Crossing. I want to be respectable, John, respectable for Will's sake."

"I don't care what you've been doing, Catherine."

Slocum slipped out of the cabin, leaving the two of them to argue over whether to tell Will's employer and his wife about Catherine's background.

"You do it? I heard shots. Where's Catherine?" asked Sara Beth, her words running together. He saw the way she looked at him, checking for injuries.

"There's no reason to drag Catherine back. She wants to stay here and thinks she has herself a good man." Slocum saw Will and Catherine moving around inside the cabin. "From what I saw, she has."

"But—"

Slocum explained everything as they rode back to the clearing where Lew had tried to rape Danielle. The dead man's horse still cropped at grass until Slocum snared the reins and fixed them to his saddle.

"You're stealing his horse?" Sara Beth asked, astounded. "You can't do that."

"It'll do me more good than it will Lew. We're going after Danielle to make sure she doesn't get herself into even more trouble."

"We're going to track her?" Sara Beth rubbed her hands together. "This is going to be fun. I've never done that before, not really. Will you show me how to do it?"

"If her trail's no harder to follow than when the four riders left the main road, you're not going to learn much."

"It might take us a while, won't it, John?"

"Might," he allowed.

"Then there'll be plenty of time for you to teach me." She smiled wickedly and added, "And there are a couple things I want to teach you."

"Danielle first," Slocum said, but his determination to find the fleeing woman and take her back to Severigne was fading as his imagination ran away with him.

They set off on the trail, but the easy tracking became more difficult when Danielle crossed a creek—or did she ride down or up it to purposefully lose any trackers? Slocum had to work to find out.

12

"I can't find her trail," Slocum admitted. He walked up and down the bank of the rapidly running stream, hunting for any sign where Danielle had left the water and taken to solid ground again.

"Did she do that on purpose?"

"Could have," Slocum said. "I don't know how she grew up. Might be she knows a lot more things than flopping onto her back."

"Don't sound so bitter, John." Sara Beth put her hand on his shoulder. "It's not all that important that you get her back to Severigne, is it?"

"Reckon not," he said. It rankled that he couldn't follow a soiled dove through territory he thought of as his own. The foothills were alive with animals and busting out with vegetation. There wasn't anything stirring here that he didn't know intimately—and he couldn't find a frightened whore fleeing from a cowboy who had tried to rape and kill her.

"She sounded like she was running for her life. That could add to her skill, couldn't it? She wouldn't necessarily get more careless."

"We ought to head back to town. I'm not looking forward to telling Severigne she lost two of her girls."

"What are you going to tell her about Catherine?"

Slocum shook his head, then smiled crookedly.

"Lost her trail, too. I reckon she's got a new name now, or will real soon. And do you see her tracks out here?" He tromped down on a carpet of pine needles. The fragrant odor of pine rose and set his pulse racing. Or was it being alone with Sara Beth out here far from all the spying eyes in town?

It didn't matter. He turned, slid his arm around her waist, and pulled her close to kiss her.

"I wondered how long it would take for you to figure that we had plenty of time for . . . not getting back to town." Sara Beth's bright blue eyes danced. She pressed even closer to him, arms around his neck. He bent again and their lips brushed lightly, then crushed in a kiss that grew in passion until Slocum knew it would be a spell before they even thought of riding back to Clabber Crossing.

"Up there," Sara Beth said. "In the sun. It's chilly here in the woods."

Cool water splattered up from the stream, turning Slocum's jeans damp. He ought to wash all his clothes, but there would be time for that after he got out of them—and found a patch of sun to spread a blanket. They walked up the hill and came out into a small glade that was about perfect. The sun slanted down, just a little past noon. The cool forest and a soft breeze kept it from being too hot here.

Then it got really hot. Slocum dropped his gun belt and Sara Beth dropped to her knees and then worked to get his fly open. One button after another popped free until finally she let out a tiny gasp. She looked up and grinned wickedly, then applied her lips to his hard organ. Slocum went weak in the knees as she sucked and licked, kissed and touched every possible spot she thought would excite him.

It all did.

He ran his hands through her long blond hair, guiding her head back and forth in a rhythm that pushed his arousal up even more. When he felt his loins beginning to burn and churn deep down, he pushed the woman back.

"No more."

"But—"

He didn't give Sara Beth a chance to protest. He lifted her up partway and then stretched her out on the blanket. Her breasts heaved under her blouse as she realized what he wanted—what she wanted, too. She unbuttoned her blouse a little bit at a time, slowly revealing the snowy white flesh hidden beneath.

As she worked to open her blouse all the way, Slocum reached under her skirt and ran his hands up the insides of her thighs, gently parting them. By the time Sara Beth had shucked out of her blouse, Slocum had bunched up her skirt around her waist.

"It's getting hot there, John," she said.

"Down there's not in the sun."

"That's not why I'm getting hot. I—" She gasped as he knelt between her opened legs and moved forward. He brushed across her nether lips with his hardness, then parted them and hid his bulbous tip just inside. She quivered and moaned softly. Her eyes closed as she reached out to him. Then she cried out in pure desire as he sank fully into her heated core.

The gentle breeze across his back and the heat at his groin drove Slocum faster until Sara Beth writhed under him, straining up to meet his every inward thrust, and then she shuddered, clawed at him, and sank back. Slocum moved faster now, then released his load in a huge rush.

He sank down atop the woman. Both of them were drenched in sweat that quickly evaporated in the sunlight and wind.

"I don't want this moment to ever end, John." She stroked over his lank hair and then wrapped her arms around him to keep him from leaving her. He wasn't inclined to do so. His brain was floating and his thoughts like the clouds growing and fading in the bright blue sky above.

He felt like a juggler in a sideshow. He had promised Severigne to help out Martin Bray, more to spy on him than to solve the problem of where the bank's money went. Owing another few weeks indentured servitude to Severigne because of a lousy poker hand didn't bother him as much as Danielle running away and Catherine finding her place in the world.

But what about Emily Dawson? He turned and looked at Sara Beth, whose eyes were closed, and a smile curled her lips as she basked in the sun. He might have found the body but knew nothing about Emily's personal life, other than she had only just come to Clabber Crossing. Everything was jumbled up but there had to be a common thread running through it all as if it were some giant tapestry. If he found that string and followed it, he could figure it all out.

Pulling on the thread would make the tapestry unravel, but causing such disarray had never bothered him before. Slocum tried to figure out why it did now. Something boiled just under the surface of an outwardly tranquil Clabber Crossing, and if he pushed too hard, it would all come spilling out. Who would be hurt wasn't obvious, but he thought Emily Dawson would be there in the boiling stew—or her family and her reputation would be. And Philomena Bray, too. She seemed a harmless woman but snooty.

As he drifted to sleep, he thought of Anna, her body sprawled on the bed upstairs in Severigne's house. Dead from too much laudanum. Suicide or murder? The same question he asked himself about Emily.

He came awake with a start when he felt a cold hand on his chest. Slocum grabbed and trapped Sara Beth's fingers on his bare chest.

"It's getting cold, John. We slept till sundown."

"We ought to find a place to hole up for the night, out of the wind." He felt the cold, wet wind and knew a storm was brewing out over the mountains and was coming this way. "I can throw together a lean-to before the storm gets here."

"Storm?"

He had barely finished lashing together the saplings to form a crude roof when the rain hit. It came down cold and wet, but they were dry enough as long as they clung to one another. Sara Beth didn't mind but Slocum grew increasingly uneasy as the storm raged through the night. He had the feeling more women would die in Clabber Crossing and he didn't know why.

When he awoke again, the fresh dawn promised a perfect day. Slocum stretched and shook Sara Beth awake.

"Time to ride. We're going back to town." He tended their horses and then ate a bit of the breakfast Sara Beth had fixed. Slocum said nothing but he was a better trail cook. Sara Beth might shine in a kitchen with an oven and all her utensils at hand but using nothing more than a pan and a low wood fire didn't highlight her culinary talents.

Three hours after noon they rode into Clabber Crossing.

"Doesn't look any different," she said. "I wonder if anybody missed me opening the restaurant."

"Missed you, is most likely," Slocum said, seeing Edgar Dawson peek around the corner of the restaurant, then disappear when Slocum noticed. The marshal made a point of coming around and so did a lot of others, and it probably wasn't so much for the grub as it was to see Sara Beth.

"I've got to tell Severigne what happened," Slocum said.

"John," Sara Beth said sharply, "you've been mighty quiet all day. You won't stop looking into how Emily died. She was a good friend. We hadn't known each other long, but she and I *were* good friends."

Slocum had decided the woman had killed herself, but he wasn't going to tell Sara Beth that. Even if Emily killed herself, there had to be some underlying reason since she had seemed a loving mother and wife and wouldn't put her family under such a dark cloud without a good reason. And why had she given him that note? That argued against suicide. Slocum's head began to hurt as he went over the reasons again that Emily might have to shoot herself.

If there ever was a good reason to kill yourself. Slocum didn't think much on that but couldn't come up with one that made sense. He valued his life too much to want to end it all by his own hand. Too many times he'd faced death and made the decision whether to let someone who hated his guts kill him—or be killed. So far, he had always chosen to be the one doing the killing.

Slocum led the two spare horses back and put them into Severigne's barn. By the time he tended them and got to the kitchen steps, the woman waited for him, hands on her hips.

"So where are they, my Danielle and Catherine?"

Slocum explained they were beyond the madam's reach now without going into too much detail when it came to Catherine. Let her try to carve out a new, different life for herself.

"But they did not die? I would not like that since I look after them so here."

"They weren't the ones who died," Slocum said, resting his hand on the butt of his six-shooter.

"Good," she said, putting the matter behind her. "I have an appointment." Severigne tipped her head to one side and waved him away, turning and hurrying into the house.

Curious, Slocum walked around the side of the building, noting the job he had done with the whitewash was barely noticeable unless you knew where to look, then poked around the side of the house in time to see Edgar Dawson running off. But it wasn't the young Peeping Tom that Severigne had gone to let inside. Slocum recognized Andrew Molinari's buckboard out front. He circled the wagon, looking into the bed, but the photographer had not come to the house for more photographs.

Slocum went to the far side of the house where Edgar had been lurking. The window was open and the lacy curtains flapped and fluttered in the breeze. Slocum pressed against the side of the house and overheard everything going on in the parlor.

"They are so good, these pictures," Severigne said. "The catalog is perfect. I can use it for selection."

"It'll speed up business, that is certain," Molinari said sardonically. "Your visitors need only look at pictures, choose, and be sent to the proper room."

"The ladies do not need to parade about downstairs," Severigne said in obvious agreement. "They do not have to all the time put on clothing and take it off."

"You are pleased with the photographs, then?"

"I am, yes . . . but what is this one? Did the lady lose her head?" Severigne laughed. Slocum had to peek inside. Severigne held up a photograph with half torn off.

"Sorry, that is one I should have discarded."

"But this one, she has a fine body. I can hire her. You can recruit using these photographs. You take pictures of potential ladies to work for me, then I hire on the basis of their looks. Before the rodeo comes to town, I can use several more girls."

"This one's not available," Molinari said.

"Pity. She has a good body for this work."

Molinari took the photograph and tucked it into an inner pocket. He and Severigne dickered some over the price, then the madam paid him. Slocum tried not to let out a low whistle when he heard how much Molinari received. Eight photographs earned him $400. He wondered if Danielle and Catherine were included, since they were no longer in Severigne's employ.

How hard would it be to remove Catherine's picture from the catalog? He didn't owe her anything but saw no reason for some drifter to come through, see the photograph, and then go to work at the Flying B and compare how the foreman's wife looked like a picture from a Clabber Crossing whorehouse. Worse, was the Flying B sending any cowboys to compete in the rodeo? It was likely at least some of those cowboys would stop by Severigne's for a night of dalliance.

It wouldn't take much for that information about their foreman's new wife to get back to Bascomb and his wife.

Getting the photograph from Severigne would be easy. She had no reason to advertise a woman whose services were not available. But getting the photographic plate from Molinari would go a ways toward keeping Catherine's new life sacrosanct.

The photographer climbed into the buckboard and rattled off toward town. Slocum had nothing to do at the moment, not with Severigne engrossed in her new catalog. He saddled his horse and cut across the field to the woods and angled into town, reaching Molinari's office before the photographer. He looked around but nobody was looking at him as he forced open the door and slipped into the studio.

The pungent smell of acid and other photographic chemicals made his eyes water. He needed some light inside but Molinari had the windows blacked out, probably to control the light as he took photographs. Slocum found the man's camera set up on a tripod and pointed at a corner of the room where black drapes had been hung. Nearby was a straight-backed chair and a footstool, other props for picture taking. In the far corner heavy curtains shut off an area for developing photographs in the absolute darkness required to prevent light damage to the plates.

Slocum quickly looked at the framed pictures on the walls and saw the different ways Molinari used the chair and footstool to pose a family. The woman sat, the husband stood behind, and children were arrayed to her left. Few variations on the composition showed up in any of the photographs. Small children were seated on the footstool and there were even a few pictures of dead men inside coffins. Slocum reckoned they must be outlaws, but he couldn't identify any of them.

Men looked different dead than alive, especially if they were riddled with bullets as several in the pictures were.

But nowhere did he find any of the photographs on display that Molinari had taken at Severigne's. Those would be kept out of sight so women wanting family portraits wouldn't be offended. Slocum looked around and found a strongbox about the right size for photographs behind the desk. He rattled the lock but it wouldn't budge. Turning the box on its side allowed the lid to open a fraction of an inch. Slocum shook the box and a sheet of paper slid out. Tugging on it, he got a look at the woman in the picture.

For a moment, he could only stare at her naked body, posed in a lewd manner that suggested she wasn't showing herself like that for the first time. He finally got a good look at the face in the photograph just as the door rattled.

Slocum hastily shoved the photograph back into the box and looked around for a place to hide.

The door opened and Molinari stepped in, a small-caliber pistol in his hand. He looked around. Slocum crouched behind the desk, his own six-shooter out. Shooting the photographer wouldn't be his choice but trying to explain how he had just happened to break into the office wasn't likely to set well with either the photographer or the marshal.

Severigne had bailed him out of jail before. He didn't want to be beholden to her yet another time. But from what he had seen in the photograph, Molinari would start shooting the instant he spotted an intruder.

For what seemed an eternity, the photographer stood in the doorway, then backed out and closed the door behind him. Slocum chanced a quick look to be sure that Molinari had left. Some rattling at the door made it sound as if the photographer had locked the door. He might have thought he had left it open, but Slocum doubted that. Molinari struck him as a methodical man who attended to details—every detail.

Not locking his office door was out of the question.

On cat's feet Slocum crossed to the far side of the room and pried back the wood shutter over the window. Molinari got into his buckboard and drove off. He might have accepted the idea that he had just forgotten to lock his office and had other business to do—or he might be going to fetch the marshal.

Slocum couldn't get out the door without ripping it off its hinges. And when he started prying away the shutter, he saw that the window had been nailed shut so no one could raise the sash.

Unless he wanted to leave an obvious trail getting out of Molinari's office, he was trapped inside . . . with the knowledge of the picture in the strongbox burning in his mind.

13

He could burn the place down. That was a desperate way to get free without Molinari knowing for sure anyone had broken into his office and seen the photograph in his strongbox, but he might as well kick out the door and take his chances. Try as he might, he couldn't pry open any of the windows. Knocking out the glass and escaping that way was about the best option open to him, but doing so would definitely alert Molinari to an intruder. Slocum wanted to make the photographer wonder if anyone had broken in rather than knowing someone had.

If he was going to bust out a window, he ought to take the strongbox with the picture with him. He could shoot off the lock and take his time looking at the rest of the contents.

Then he saw the way out. At the far end of the room a stovepipe rose to the ceiling. The spot where the pipe went through the roof had been crudely plastered. Slocum jumped to the top of the iron stone and ran his fingers under the plaster, which came loose in a giant chunk. He let it fall, then reached up, grabbed the exposed roof through the hole, and pulled hard. He kicked free and worked his way through the hole onto the roof. It was a tight fit and he left a bit of skin behind but he managed to flop facedown on the roof so he could look back into Molinari's office. The only trace that the plaster hadn't fallen on its own were his boot prints on the top of the iron stove.

Working quickly, he pried loose more of the plaster and carefully dropped it onto the stove to cover the prints. Only when he was sure no one could tell that the roof simply hadn't given way due to a bad repair job did he scoot back and go to the far side of the roof. He saw Molinari and the marshal coming back. He jumped from the roof, hit the ground hard, and rolled, coming to his feet. Several quick paces took him behind the next building and out of sight. He wasted no time making a beeline for Sara Beth's restaurant.

He didn't bother with the front door. Customers came and went already. He slipped into the kitchen and was hit with a blast of heat from the cooking stove. He was covered with plaster dust so he set about washing his face and hands. He skinned out of his coat and vest, wiped them down the best he could, and then shucked off his shirt to rinse it out in a pan of water beside the sink.

"Oh my God!"

Slocum reached for his six-shooter, then went back to cleaning up.

"What have you been up to, John? I've got a full restaurant out there, and I can't have you parading around half naked." Sara Beth stopped, pursed her lips, then said, "Well, I *could* but folks would talk."

"They'd gossip," Slocum corrected. He wrung out his shirt and held it near the stove. The heat made quick work of drying. With Sara Beth's help, he put it back on.

"You look more presentable. What did you do? Get yourself tangled up with a dust devil? No, that couldn't be. This is white powder."

"Don't worry your pretty head about it," he told her.

"I've got customers to serve." She gathered plates of food and put them on a tray. Slocum stopped her.

"Before you go, was Emily ever in Kansas City?"

"Why, yes, she was. She must have been since she came west from Ohio."

"But she married Henry in Ohio?"

"She said she did." Sara Beth stared at him. "What's this all about?"

"Go feed your customers." He gave her a quick kiss and a swat on the bottom to send her on her way. Only when she had disappeared into the main dining room did he put on his vest and coat, wiping off the last specks of plaster. Even if the marshal figured out who had broken into Molinari's office, there wasn't any proof.

"Proof," he muttered under his breath. Slocum stepped outside and went straight for the church, where Henry Dawson was preparing for the Wednesday night prayer meeting.

The preacher looked up. A flash of irritation at the intrusion vanished, and he smiled and held out his hand. Slocum shook it.

"You've come to join us tonight, Mr. Slocum? This is something of a surprise."

"I just wanted a question answered."

"Just one? Your life is blessed if there is only one. And it will be even more blessed if I can give you the answer."

Before the preacher started on a sermon, Slocum cut him off.

"Where in Ohio did you marry your wife?"

Henry Dawson looked confused, then said, "You must mean where did Emily come from. She came from Ohio, but we met in Kansas City and were married there. Her people all died in a diphtheria epidemic, but by God's mercy she escaped. She couldn't bear to remain where so many of her family rested in graves, so she left Ohio. It was my good fortune that she had yet to travel on. She was on her way to New Orleans."

"You know why?"

Henry Dawson smiled wanly.

"She thought it provided more opportunity for her, but I proved her wrong."

"You came here from Kansas City?"

"Oh, no, we started a mission in Indian Territory but decided our true calling was farther west, so we moved on. When we reached Clabber Crossing, found it didn't have a pastor, we knew we had found our destiny."

"Thanks, Reverend," Slocum said as he turned to leave. He knew that the town's need for a minister was only part of the reason they had stayed there. They had run out of money to go any farther west.

"You can stay for my sermon. It's going to be a rousing one about . . ."

Slocum didn't hear the rest. He plunged out into the twilight and went directly back to Severigne's. Her customers—the ones not intending to go to the prayer meeting—were already starting to file in. Then Slocum had a cynical thought that the men were coming early tonight so they could have a good tumble in the hay before they had to go hear the reverend's sermon.

"There you are. What have you been doing? I have need of you already this night. Drunks! Pah! I would stop all sale of whiskey. It makes you men rowdy or rough. I am not sure which is worse."

"I need to talk to you."

"First, the drunk. Throw him the hell out!"

Slocum was burning with the need to ask Severigne a few questions but went into the parlor, where the drunk man had trapped Alice and held her in the corner so she couldn't escape. She looked past the man and silently implored Slocum to do something. He ignored everyone else in the room, and Severigne had a goodly number tonight, grabbed the man by the collar, and lifted him up onto his toes.

Off-balance, the man staggered. Slocum steered him down the hall to the kitchen, where Severigne held open the screen door. Slocum never slowed his bum's rush and the man hit the steps and fell heavily. Only then did he release his collar so he wouldn't be pulled along after him. Hopping down to stand beside the man as he struggled to get up, Slocum grabbed his collar again and helped him along to the watering trough.

A tiny geyser exploded when Slocum shoved the man's head under. He struggled, sputtered, and began blowing bubbles. When the bubbles stopped, Slocum yanked him up and let him fall to the ground.

"When you learn how to treat a lady, you can come back. Take my advice and do it sober."

"Lady? Lady? She's a whore. She ain't no—"

Slocum held him under a trifle longer this time. When he released him, the man spit out half a lungful of water.

"Awright, I'll go. Which way's town?"

Slocum got him on the road into Clabber Crossing, where he'd either go back to drinking and probably brag about how good he was in bed or find himself another soiled dove. It didn't matter to Slocum as long as he kept his business somewhere else and caused trouble a long ways away.

He returned to the house to find Severigne sitting at the kitchen table drinking straight from a bottle of wine. She dropped it to the table with a loud clack and looked up at him.

"Some nights I wish to be a farmer's wife. Even a rancher's! Like Catherine."

Slocum looked at her hard. Severigne smiled slyly and told him, "I am not without my sources of information. Let her go. *You* let her go. Pah! It is for the best. She was not cut out for this life."

"You haven't heard anything about Danielle, have you?" When Severigne shook her head and took another drink straight from the bottle, Slocum asked the question that had been burning him up since he barely got out of Molinari's office without being caught. "Did you know Emily Dawson when she was in Kansas City?"

Severigne frowned.

"I did not."

"What about Philomena?"

"Bray's wife? That Philomena? No, I did not know her before seeing her here in town. This is a strange question you ask, Slocum. What progress have you made finding who is stealing from the bank?"

"Not a great deal," Slocum said. He sat where he could look down the hall and catch sight of a narrow section of the parlor. Alice and her teller sat on the love seat, heads together. Could they be in cahoots? The teller would steal to impress Alice, but Slocum had asked around and Alice wasn't any better off than the other Cyprians working for Severigne. If she had even a dime more, she would have either lorded it over the others or taken the money and moved on to a bigger city to spend her newfound wealth. The teller hardly seemed the type to embezzle, except to impress a woman.

"You have a strange look about you. What have you uncovered?"

"Might be nothing, but I'm beginning to wonder. Did Molinari show you any photographs he'd taken of other whores?"

"Of course. He has worked widely throughout the West. He is very good at his job." She fixed him with a steady stare but he ignored her. His mind raced as he put tiny facts together. Kansas City seemed like the center of the canker Severigne wanted him to lance—and she had no idea about it. For all that, he had only suspicions.

"You would go out again tonight? Business is slowing. The preacher man has drained many of my best customers—after my girls drained them, of course!" Severigne laughed. "We tend the body and the reverend tends their soul. This is a busy night for all of us."

"I'll be back before midnight to make sure everyone's left."

"I might change the rule and let some stay until morning. For a price, of course. There might be more money in it for both the house and the girls." Severigne hummed to herself as she took a piece of foolscap and began making intricate calculations. Slocum left the madam to her figures and fetched his horse, riding back to town rather than walking.

He wasn't sure if he'd have to make a quick escape. Andrew Molinari was a suspicious cuss, and the marshal would take special delight in clapping him into jail again, this time throwing away the key.

Slocum chuckled as he thought of the people lined up to get him out. Not only would Severigne and Clabber demand his release but Martin Bray would, too, hoping that Slocum could find his thief.

If things went well, Slocum figured to know who stole the money from the bank before sunrise. He rode past the row of saloons doing subdued business and then past the bank. The road from here curved around the hill and went up to the Bray house atop the hill. Slocum wanted a word with Philomena. If she had gone to the prayer meeting, he could stop her on the way home so her husband would never know they had spoken.

Before he had ridden twenty yards along the trail, he heard the rattle of a buggy coming toward him. He veered from the road and sat astride his horse in deep shadows as Philomena drove past. Either she had left Reverend Dawson's sermon early or she hadn't gone at all. The expression of determination on her face warned Slocum that he might have a blowup on his hands. He followed her buggy as she drove straight for Molinari's office.

She jumped to the ground and walked fast to the office door. Philomena Bray didn't bother knocking; she pushed in and slammed the door behind her. Slocum was quick to follow. He knew the windows were boarded up and nailed shut so he risked pressing his ear against the door panel. Faint words became more distinct as Philomena began shouting.

". . . this is all, I won't give you another cent!"

"They are so lovely, those legs of yours. And your naked breasts."

The woman let out a shriek of rage, and Slocum chanced opening the door a crack to peer inside. Philomena clawed at Molinari's face, but the photographer shoved her back and held up the photograph Slocum had seen in the strongbox.

"What would your loving husband say if he saw this? Why, I could sell copies to the soldiers at the army post. They would have your naked glory displayed for every last one to see. Horse soldiers, Philomena, common soldiers just like the ones you used to—"

"Shut up! Shut up!" The woman burst into tears. "I can't pay any more. There's no more money in the bank. I've stolen it all."

"Oh, my dear, not all," said Molinari. "There must be some left. Enough for you to give to me." His voice hardened. "Five thousand more and the photos are all yours to do with as you please. Refuse to get me the money and your lovely face—your naked body—will be seen by not only your husband but every man in Wyoming."

"I should never have let you take that picture."

"Why not? It was good advertising for that brothel where you worked. You seem so cheerful in the photograph, also. Some of the *joie de vivre* has fled your life."

"I hate you."

"I could care less," Molinari said. "One month. You have one month to get me the money, and I don't care how you do it. You might go back to your old profession. I hear Severigne lost a couple of her sluts and the rodeo will be in town soon. Think of all those eager cowboys wanting something under them other than their horses. It would be like old times for you."

Slocum pulled the door shut and slipped around the side of the building as Philomena burst out, sobbing bitterly. She climbed into her buggy, caught her breath, then snapped the reins, getting the horse pulling her back in the direction of the house on the hill.

Slocum felt no satisfaction finding who was stealing the bank's money. Philomena had access in some way, possibly to the account books her husband left lying around. Paying off a blackmailer was never the smart thing to do, but he saw her problem. A woman of her social stature would be ruined if photographs of her naked were widely distributed. It would ruin her and her husband.

He circled the building to get his horse but saw two men standing beside it. His Colt Navy slid from his holster, but he hesitated when he heard one say, "This belongs to that owlhoot we ambushed."

"I told you we should have finished him off. He musta knowed you killed that whore."

"I didn't leave anything behind. She scratched me, but so what? For all the damned undertaker said, ever'one thinks she died of too much opium—just like I intended."

"You shouldna got involved with her."

"I couldn't have her talkin' 'bout the pictures."

"You were dumb to show her Molinari's stash like that. He'll kill you if he finds out you took 'em."

"Borrowed. That's all I done. I put 'em back. But what about the cowboy? We kin wait for him to fetch his horse and cut him down."

"He put up too much of a fight before. He's one tough hombre."

"You had a rifle. You shoulda killed him with your first shot."

"You didn't do anything to help."

"We can get him now. He's got to be around somewhere, snooping about. I heard tell he went to work for Severigne."

"Just what we need—him, the dead whore, and Severigne. Get your rifle. If you get down over by the shed, you can finish him once and for all. I'll go tell the boss we got company."

"Don't tell him we suspect it's the son of a bitch working for Severigne. He'll hit the ceiling."

"Don't worry. I'm not as dumb as you." The man hurried away muttering about fooling around with whores.

Slocum wasn't surprised when the one man went inside Molinari's office, but he couldn't get to his horse with the other man—the one who had tried to ambush him when he first got to town—hunkered down by the shed. From there the man had an easy shot no matter how Slocum approached his horse.

He had found out not only who had murdered Anna but also what Martin Bray needed to know. This would sate Severigne's insatiable appetite for gossip, too, but he wasn't about to let these back shooters keep his horse by simply walking away.

Whatever he did had to be done fast before the second gunman returned. Slocum came to a decision fast and stepped out in plain sight. He heard the sniper's rifle click as a round was jacked into the chamber, but he stepped out, hoping his scheme worked. If it didn't, he was a dead man.

14

"You got whiskey," Slocum slurred as he stumbled toward the hidden sniper, keeping his head down and half turned away. "Just wanna drink. Mighty dry. Like a desert down my throat."

"Git on out of here, you damned drunk. You—"

The ambusher rose and waved for Slocum to move on. Slocum was close enough to wrest the rifle from his hand and swing it around. He aimed the stock at the man's head but connected instead with his knee because both of them were moving and fighting. This was good enough to make the man let out a yelp, grab his kneecap, and give Slocum the chance to plant a hard fist on the point of the chin. The man folded like a bad poker hand.

Slocum threw aside the rifle and vaulted into the saddle, riding off before the man's partner could get out of the office to see what caused the ruckus. A bullet sang through the air over his head, but Slocum was far enough away that a pistol shot would have to be luckier than skillful to hit him. He got a good look at the man he had knocked out but doubted the man could identify him.

They knew him, though. They had tried to kill him when

he had first come to Clabber Crossing. He hadn't suspected Molinari of anything then—hadn't even known Molinari existed since the photographer was out making the rounds of the ranches plying his trade. But thinking he knew about their role in faking Anna's suicide would cause them to single him out to be killed.

Slocum wanted to ride back to Severigne and tell her what he had learned but somehow going to see Sara Beth appealed more. He was reaching the point where Clabber Crossing was getting too dangerous for him. His life had been spent drifting, sometimes because of the men he had pissed off but usually because he had grown tired of the sameness and routine and had sought more excitement. There was no question excitement had found him here at the western edge of Wyoming, and he wasn't sure he wanted to deal with it right now.

He dismounted behind the restaurant and went into the kitchen. It was as hot as before, but he heard the clank of dishes out in the dining room and knew the last of the customers had left. Sara Beth was cleaning up. When she came into the kitchen with an armload of dirty plates, she let out a yelp and almost dropped the stack.

"John, stop hiding like that. You scared the life out of me."

"You look pretty lively to me."

"My heart's banging away like a smithy's hammer on an anvil."

"More than usual when you see me?" he joshed.

"Oh, you. Make it up to me. Start washing dishes."

"I have to get back to Severigne's," he said. He had washed more than his share of dishes in his day and wasn't inclined to help Sara Beth with her chores.

"I'll make it worth your while," she said, batting her eyelashes in his direction.

"I've got a couple gunmen hot on my trail. They missed killing me a few minutes ago, and if I stay, they'll find me for sure. I don't want you getting shot up."

"Are you joking?" Sara Beth stared hard at him. "You're not! Turn them in to the marshal. Dunbar is a worthless carbuncle on this town's backside, but he has to enforce the law sometimes."

"I'm not sure who's being paid off, but the owlhoots after me have had it in for me since I came to town. Now they have even more reason."

"Start washing and I'll tell you what I found out from Jacob."

"Who's he?"

Sara Beth looked away, then heaved a deep sigh. She was working on telling him something unpleasant. The woman finally worked up her courage.

"Jacob is the town telegrapher. Him and me, well, before you rode into town, we—"

"What did Jacob have to tell you that's so important?" Slocum didn't care about Sara Beth's love life before he had come to town, and he supposed she would continue with the telegrapher after he left. She had roots in Clabber Crossing and he didn't—he never would. Jacob, though, was an important citizen in town, connecting everyone with the world outside Wyoming.

"I asked him to send a wire to the Western Union operator in Kansas City."

Slocum perked up. He started scraping the dishes and handing them to her to wash. What Sara Beth built up to tell him might be worth a few cleaned plates and cups.

"He—the telegrapher in Kansas City—frequented a cathouse and remembered a woman who matched Emily's description. The time was about right, too, for when she was getting married to Henry. The telegrapher had her picked out as his favorite and one night she was gone. Another girl said she had run off to marry a preacher."

"There might be a lot of hookers with dark hair matching Emily's description."

"He said she had a long scar on the right side of her body. It ran from her armpit down to her hip. Big scar, vivid pink." Sara Beth swallowed hard and pointedly ignored his eyes. "I think Emily had a scar like that. I'm not sure but . . . she might have," she finished lamely.

"That would be a pretty decent way of identifying her," Slocum said.

"What? Dig her up and look to be sure?"

"Cooper. That's the undertaker's name, isn't it?" Sara Beth nodded. "I can ask. He prepared the body for burial and would have seen a scar that big."

"Jacob's friend said Emily—or whoever—told him she got it when she fell on a disc harrow as a child and almost died. Her ma stitched her up but it left the scar. That was about all she ever shared with him about her life."

"They were on business terms, not personal," Slocum said.

"I reckon."

They washed dishes in silence for a while, then Sara Beth said, "If it's true that Emily lied about her background, what should I do, John? I ought to tell the preacher."

"Why? Does it change how he felt about her? It might change the way he remembers her—him and their son."

"You'd keep it quiet?"

"It's not my business, and as you said, it might be somebody else. Without a photograph, how would we ever be sure?" As he spoke, a cold knot formed in the pit of his stomach. *Without a photograph.* What if Molinari had such a picture? He'd blackmailed Philomena Bray. Philomena and Emily might not have worked at the same brothel but an enterprising photographer like Molinari would shop his catalog idea around to all the whorehouses. He kept the plates so he could make more photos and use them later. He had admitted selling such pictures to the soldiers during the war.

There wasn't anything to stop him from blackmailing more than one woman who was trying to better herself by marrying up and hiding her background.

"Would you ask Henry Dawson about the scar?"

Sara Beth looked at him directly for the first time and shook her head adamantly.

"I will not. There is no way I could be discreet about such a question. Hasn't the man suffered enough? As you said, why is it important now? Poor Emily's dead."

Slocum had reason to think she had killed herself, but what if she hadn't? He wasn't going to let Molinari get away with murder—or telling his henchmen to kill Emily and make it appear to be suicide like they had with Anna.

"You're right," Slocum said. "There's no reason." He put the last of the platters down and wiped his hands on a towel. "I've got to go."

"No, John. Stay. You don't have to go back to that horrible place. Severigne would never hold it against you if you just up and took off."

Slocum laughed harshly. Severigne would do just such a thing. She was a businesswoman who kept her employees in line. More than that, Slocum's word was on the line. He had promised Clabber and Severigne. He still had a couple weeks to go before his gambling debt was paid off.

"I'm not running away. I'll be back later, unless you and your telegrapher are sending messages to each other in bed."

"John, I—never mind."

She didn't try to kiss him, and he simply tossed the hand towel onto the table and left. He thought he heard Sara Beth crying but wasn't sure—and wasn't sure it mattered. He rode back to Severigne's but had come to a decision before he reached the house.

He rummaged through the shed and found a shovel. What he intended to do was illegal and immoral, and if he hadn't worried about it before, he would now since he could burn in hell forever. It took him a while to ride outside town and find Primrose Hill, where the cemetery spread out over a knoll overlooking the prairie to the east. Slocum tethered his horse some distance from the cemetery and walked through the gravestones. The Masonic section sported decent headstones with names and dates engraved. The portion adjoining had been reserved for prominent folks, still with stone markers. Farther along, in a section fenced off with a knee-high rail, was the ordinary people's section. More often than not a wood plank had been carved with the name of the deceased.

Beyond that, but higher on the hill, he found Emily Dawson's grave. The earth had yet to sink back down and compact above her body. He looked around, just to be sure nobody spied on him. Why should they? He was out in the cemetery long after sundown. Most townspeople wouldn't stray out here for any reason, whether they were scared of haints or simply respected the resting place of a loved one.

He dug. It took him longer than he'd expected to get down to the pine box and brush off the dirt. The odor of decay rose even with the lid closed, but Slocum knew what he had to do. He sucked in his breath, held it, and then pried open the coffin. A gust of grave fumes hit him although he had expected it and had closed his eyes. When his lungs felt like bursting, he exhaled slowly, pulled up his bandanna, and sucked in timid breaths through it.

Slocum dropped down, gripped the corpse's arm, and tugged. It came off. Muttering a curse under his breath, he used the shovel to roll Emily Dawson's remains to one side, exposing her right rib cage. The flesh was wrinkled and partly eaten by worms, but in the moonlight he saw a long scar running from her armpit down to her hip.

The Kansas City whore and Emily Dawson were one and the same. Slocum didn't believe in coincidence, and the telegrapher had been too specific about the scar for there to be two women with similar disfigurement. Slocum closed the lid and shoveled back the dirt. Tamping it down so it looked as it had before he dug her up proved impossible, so he didn't bother.

As he walked back to his horse, he saw something move

within the shadows ahead of him. He drew and aimed, but the wavering shadow disappeared and left him only with the burden of what he had just done.

Slocum rode slowly back toward town, not sure how he could use any of the information he had unearthed. At that thought, he wiped his hands against his jeans, leaving dirty streaks. He had uncovered more than a few hidden facts about Emily Dawson and Philomena Bray. He wished he could have gone to the undertaker and gotten a decent answer but knew better than to ask. His question would be on everyone's lips for fifty miles around.

He didn't want the preacher to find out about his wife. But that thought rankled. He might not owe anything to the man or the memory of his wife, but Slocum wondered if Emily had killed herself. The reverend might have put the gun to her head and pulled the trigger because he had discovered everything that Slocum had.

It didn't pay to think too long on such things. It made his head hurt—and without finishing off a pint of whiskey to get there.

He rode up to the house and dismounted, noting a buggy out front he didn't recognize. Slocum went in the rear and walked softly to a point where he could listen in as Severigne talked to her late-night visitor.

"Is this something you would do?" Severigne asked.

Slocum stood a little straighter when he recognized Henry Dawson's voice.

"It is unusual but I might see my way to doing as you ask. I would need more assurance that it would not become a mockery."

"A moment, Reverend," Severigne said. Louder, she called, "Mr. Slocum, you should be involved in our negotiation."

Slocum went into the parlor. The pastor sat stiff as a board across the table from Severigne, holding a cup of tea. He looked as uncomfortable as . . . a preacher in a whorehouse.

"Good evening," Slocum said, aware that the dirt on his shirt and hands had come from the grave of the man's wife.

"Reverend Dawson has agreed to conduct a wedding service out front."

"Who's getting married?" Slocum stared at Severigne, wondering if she was playing some elaborate game that he wasn't privy to.

"Since Catherine found herself a husband on a nearby ranch, the other girls have been chattering like magpies. Missy wants to marry the owner of the H Bar L and I have agreed."

"It smacks of slavery, this way you're dickering with the rancher," muttered Dawson.

"Nonsense. It is traditional for a dowry to be offered."

"The rancher wants only the best for his future wife. Missy wouldn't feel right simply riding off."

"Like Catherine," Slocum said. He wondered if Severigne and Missy had conspired to take the owner of the H Bar L for some money and this was part of the hoax. Having the reverend involved would make it seem on the level.

"She was such a strong-headed girl. Not like Missy, who wants to observe the niceties of marital bliss."

"You'll perform the ceremony?" Slocum looked straight at Henry Dawson, who reluctantly nodded.

"I'm about the only one who can marry them, other than the circuit judge. He won't be through Clabber Crossing for another month and there seems to be some urgency to the wedding."

Things fell into place for Slocum. Missy was pregnant and had landed herself an honorable man, though who the father might be would always be open to question. This wasn't something all that rare.

"I will get the money from the rancher and we will put on a fine wedding," Severigne said, as if everything was settled.

"There will be details," Henry Dawson said. His uneasiness with the arrangements was evident. He stood to leave.

Out of the corner of his eye, Slocum caught movement at the window. He turned and drew, not intending to let Molinari's gunmen cut him down from ambush.

"Wait!" Dawson said, holding out his hand. "That's my son. He came with me. Don't shoot, Mr. Slocum. Please."

"He is a fine boy. Perhaps he can be the ring bearer at the wedding," Severigne said.

Slocum slipped his six-shooter back into the holster. Edgar Dawson had a habit of looking through windows all over town. What had he seen? Slocum would have to ask—when his father wasn't around.

15

Tracking Edgar Dawson proved harder than Slocum had anticipated. The boy was fast, and he knew the woods around town better than Slocum ever could. Twice Slocum found likely spots where the boy had stopped, possibly to rest. He found partially eaten bread in the crook of a tree and small, shiny stones polished by a running creek in the bole of another tree. But the boy might as well have turned into a rabbit and hopped into his burrow for all the luck Slocum had finding him.

Slocum ended up near the cabin where he had found Emily Dawson's body. He had gone through the debris there several times and hadn't come up with any likely killer. The more he thought on it, the more likely it seemed that Emily had killed herself rather than submit to Molinari's blackmail. As a pastor's wife, she didn't have anywhere near the financial resources that Philomena Bray had.

He ought to tell Bray he had discovered the embezzler but couldn't find it in his heart to do so—not yet. What would it gain having Martin Bray kill his wife, and Slocum knew that would be the outcome. Bray wasn't a man who took financial loss easily. Coming to Slocum for help proved that. Slocum didn't owe any of them a plugged nickel, but what stuck in his craw was the way Molinari worked. Blackmailing women trying to make their lives outside a whorehouse was about as despicable as it got.

After poking through the cabin again, he finally sat in the chair where Emily had died. He stared ahead as she must have. Why had she given him that note if all she wanted to do was kill herself? A hardness seized his heart and rage mounted as he thought it through. He was new in town and was obviously of low moral character since he had been sent out to a whorehouse to work off a gambling debt.

Emily had wanted it to look as if he had killed her. Suicide caused too many questions to be asked, and answers were what she wanted to avoid. But if a drifter shot her, it might appear that she had tried to defend herself against his unwanted sexual advances. It didn't matter if he was hanged for the crime. Her reputation would be intact. She wouldn't be a whore blackmailed by an unscrupulous photographer. She would be the preacher's wife defending her honor—her family—against a sexual predator. Emily Dawson would be a hero, not a woman trying to run from a sordid past that was rapidly overtaking her.

That also explained why Marshal Dunbar had been so close. Although he had never said, Emily must have sent him a note, too, so that the lawman would find Slocum by her body and seal his guilt. Her timing had been off and she had killed herself before either Slocum or the marshal could hear the killing gunshot.

Slocum didn't like it but had to admit she was clever. Protecting her husband and son mattered more than an innocent man getting his neck stretched.

He wondered what Molinari would have done if her plan had succeeded. As far as Slocum could tell, the photographer would have done nothing. Emily would have won. There was no reason Molinari would come forward with his photographs because it might give Slocum an argument to present to the jury: she was nothing but a whore. On the other hand, if Molinari came forward with the photographs, he would have had to explain how he had come by them. Worse, the leverage he held over Philomena Bray might vanish.

Pushing out of the rickety chair, Slocum left the cabin, never wanting to return here again. He had worked out part of the secrets flowing just under the calm surface of Clabber Crossing. Others were still hidden from him, but he knew they all had a common source.

Andrew Molinari.

He returned to Severigne's house to find it bustling with activity. He was not in the mood to deal with the madam or her clients but found he had no choice.

"Slocum, come here. Now." Severigne motioned imperiously. When he got to the foot of the kitchen steps, she came down and said in a low voice, "I need your experience."

"For what?"

"The rancher is here. He negotiates, but I find I cannot understand all he says. You are a cowboy. You know these things."

"I can't negotiate for a woman's hand in marriage. That's between Missy and the rancher."

"His name is Lehrer, and I must know if he is, how do you say it, on the up-and-up."

"Folks in town must know if he owns a ranch anywhere nearby. Ask them."

"I . . . I trust you." The words were almost as if they burned Severigne's tongue to say. "Those in town look down their big noses at me and what I do here. You do not."

"Sometimes I've taken a dip in a pond like this and gotten more than my toes wet. Maybe not as fancy, but I'm not going to deny it."

"You must ask him of cow things. You know this. Do it for my sake. Do it for Missy."

"Either she loves him or she doesn't. That goes for this

Lehrer. The number of head he runs or how big the spread shouldn't matter."

"As long as her spread is big enough for him, eh?"

"I'll talk to him. Might be I can get a job when I finish here." He followed Severigne into the house, knowing a job would be the last thing he'd ever ask Lehrer for. He couldn't imagine working for Missy. She was conniving and almost as much a moneygrubber as Severigne, only lacking the madam's finesse.

"This the gent you told me about?" A whipcord thin man stood and thrust out his hand. Slocum wasn't surprised at the powerful grip or the calluses. This wasn't a rancher who sat in a fancy house and let his cowboys do the work. He got out and rode herd with them. He was an inch or two shorter than Slocum's six feet and his sandy hair was already going thin, although he couldn't have been thirty. His face was like tanned leather, and his pale gray eyes weren't missing a thing.

"He is. Mr. Lehrer."

"Call me Hans. All my boys do."

"Hans, such a fine Old World name." Severigne told some meaningless story about France.

Lehrer smiled politely and said, "You got me about that, Miss Severigne. I was born down in New Braunfals and sorta made my way north."

"Been here long?" Slocum asked. He had no idea what Severigne wanted him to find out.

"A couple years. Gets mighty lonely up here. I run a thousand head of cattle, and even with a dozen cowboys workin' the herd, it gets lonely, if you know what I mean."

"Reckon so," Slocum said. "You visit Missy often?"

"Not as often as I'd like, which is why I asked her to marry me."

"You don't have any problem with her being a whore?"

"Slocum!" Severigne sounded outraged, but her shrewd eyes took in Lehrer's every twitch and tic and expression.

Slocum vowed never to play poker with her. With the luck he'd had since coming to Clabber Crossing, he ought to swear off gambling altogether.

"Please, Miss Severigne, that's a fair question. My people aren't the most law-abiding down in Texas, which is one reason I came to Wyoming. But I put that life behind me, and Missy says she can put this behind her, too."

"Not everything I've learned here, Hans." Missy giggled like a schoolgirl. "And I won't forget all the things *you* taught me."

"See? She's a frisky little filly and the best damned liar this side of the Tetons."

"Hans!" Missy feigned outrage, but Slocum saw she was pleased. It came as something of a surprise to him, but he thought the two of them might actually be in love.

A sharp rap at the front door caused Severigne to look irritated, then she hurried over and opened it. Slocum saw past her to one of Molinari's gunman. He shot to his feet, hand going to his six-shooter, but Severigne had already closed the door and was coming back.

Slocum passed her, threw open the door, and saw the man riding off at a gallop. He considered going after him, but what was the point?

He closed the door as Severigne handed Missy a note. Her face went pale, then she flushed.

"I have to go. Just for a moment," she said.

"Is there something wrong?" Slocum asked. She pushed past him without looking at him. She looked as if she might cry at any instant or perhaps kill someone.

"Slocum, here," Severigne said, patting the chair he had vacated. He returned but wondered what was in the note Missy had taken with her, clutched in her fist.

"We can settle this matter," Hans Lehrer said. "What'll it take for you to agree to let me and Missy get hitched?"

Severigne smiled, but before she could say a word, Slocum interrupted. "You go on. I'll be back in a minute." He had caught sight of Missy riding off in the direction taken by Molinari's henchman. Ignoring Severigne's protest, he got to his horse and rode after Missy. She had a few minutes' head start but was galloping hard enough to tire her mount within a mile. Slocum maintained a more sedate pace, trotting along as he kept a sharp lookout. Molinari's men had tried to ambush him twice. He didn't intend to let them have a third shot at him.

Missy must have realized she was killing her horse because she slowed but kept moving faster than Slocum wanted to push his own horse. She knew where she was headed and he didn't, though the dark allowed him to ride closer than he could have in the daytime. Something told him that she would veer away from her rendezvous if she thought she was being trailed.

That she didn't bother to look behind told Slocum she was in a powerful hurry, and all because of the note.

He kept riding, then stopped abruptly because he no longer heard the woman's horse ahead. Slocum turned slowly and caught faint voices drifting on the night air. He rode slowly in that direction, moving through a ravine and up into a wooded area until he caught sight of two figures silhouetted by the moonlight. Only then did he dismount and advance on foot, straining to hear what was being said.

"You stop meddling. This is none of your business!" Missy came within an inch of shouting.

"I'm not meddling. I want to offer the groom a fine picture of his betrothed."

Slocum recognized Molinari's voice even if he couldn't make out the man's face. The moonlight reflected off a shiny photograph as the photographer moved closer to Missy. The woman recoiled as if she had been struck.

"Go on. Look at it and tell me if this isn't what a fine, upstanding rancher would frame and hang on the wall to commemorate his nuptials."

Missy snatched the photograph from Molinari and held

it up to study it. All Slocum saw was the back of the photograph. At more than twenty feet, he wouldn't have been able to make out the details even in broad daylight.

"No, you—you're a horrible man! You wouldn't show Hans this!" Missy ripped up the photo and threw it at Molinari's feet. The photographer knelt and carefully picked up the pieces and tucked them into his coat pocket.

"We wouldn't want some curious cowboy to see the pieces. Why, even the torn sections are so—"

"I'll kill you!"

"My assistants have orders to show this photo and quite a few others of you to anyone in town who'd like to see them. Kill me and you'll be exposed." Molinari chuckled. "I'd say you'll be exposed more than you are in that photograph."

"Go to hell!"

"You know what I want," Molinari called after her as Missy rushed off, mounted, and rode into the night.

Slocum hesitated. He could trail Molinari, probably back to his office, and find what that photograph was by either stealing it or beating the information out of the photographer. Since Lehrer knew what his bride-to-be did for a living, what could Molinari have shown Missy to upset her so? Slocum believed the photographer when he said he had more copies—as many copies as he wanted. From what Slocum knew of the photographic process, as long as Molinari had the original plate, he could make all the photographs he liked. The process was something akin to magic as far as Slocum could tell, but the photographer didn't need any single printed photograph when he could flood the town with hundreds of copies.

Slocum had no doubt Molinari would carry through with his threat. If what he had figured out about Emily was right, Molinari had driven her to suicide. And there was no doubt about him blackmailing Philomena Bray. But what could Molinari possibly have photographed with Missy in the picture to make her react the way she had?

He came to a quick decision. Molinari's henchmen probably waited not far off to protect their boss. Taking on all three in the dark of the night, even with the moon to help him a mite, wasn't smart. He had the advantage of surprise, but that would only bring down one of the men and then he would be pitted against two.

If either got away, Missy's photograph would be spread around town. Slocum wanted to keep that from happening.

He backed away, then got his horse and rode at an angle to the way he had approached the meeting. His tactic worked. Missy had swung about in a wide circle before heading back to Severigne's. He spotted her only a little bit ahead and yelled.

The woman put down her head and urged her horse on to greater speed.

"Missy, it's me, Slocum. Wait!" Either she didn't hear or she didn't believe him. He rode after her until his horse tired fast and he found himself walking along, picking his way through grassy stretches until he finally found a road. Getting his bearings, he went to Clabber Crossing and then on to Severigne's. Missy had beaten him there by quite a stretch.

As he rode up, he saw Missy and Hans Lehrer lighted in the parlor. They argued, but he couldn't hear the words. He tethered his horse and went in the front door, almost colliding with Severigne.

"Where have you gone? She has gone insane. Crazy. She had taken the loco weed! Smoked it. Eaten it!"

Slocum heard Missy and Lehrer and knew right away what the fight was over.

"Why not, sweetheart? I love you. I don't give two hoots and a holler if you worked in every cathouse between here and the Mississippi."

"You don't want me. You just think you do. I'm not maryin' you, Hans Lehrer. Not in a million years."

Slocum almost called out asking what Molinari had shown her, but that wouldn't do any of them any good.

"If you were a bloody-handed murderer, I'd still love you."

"You don't know what you're talking about. You don't. Get out of here. I'm not marrying you and that's all I got to say!"

Missy pushed past the rancher, looked stricken at Severigne and Slocum, then ran up the stairs, crying.

"Come back here, Missy. I want some answers!"

Slocum stopped Lehrer as he tried to follow Missy up the stairs.

"Let her simmer down," Slocum suggested. Lehrer reached into his shirt pocket and pulled out a wad of greenbacks large enough to choke a cow.

"I'm buyin' time with her."

"No, no," Severigne said, shaking her head. She stared hard at the money. Slocum knew how difficult it was for the madam to turn down this much folding money, but she did. "She is distraught. You will come back another time."

"I'm marrying her. Mark my words, I am!" With that, Lehrer stormed from the house, slamming the door hard enough to rattle the knickknacks on the table across the room.

"What has happened? Where did she go?"

Slocum didn't feel like answering Severigne because he didn't have any idea what had happened when Missy had met Molinari. But he was going to find out.

16

"You stand there and draw," Randall Bray said, squinting because he had foolishly come out into Main Street, facing the rising sun as he called out Slocum. His face was all thunderclouds, and lightning shot from his eyes. Shoulders tensed and rocked forward on the balls of his feet, he looked unbalanced enough to simply push over, but Slocum took the threat seriously. Slocum saw that his hand also trembled as it poised above the six-shooter at his hip.

"You clean your gun this time?" Slocum asked. All around, men and women ducked inside, wanting to get out of the line of fire if a gunfight started. Slocum noticed that nobody went to fetch the marshal. Good. He could take care of this himself.

"You're not gonna weasel out of this. I'm calling you out!"

Slocum stared at the young man, then asked, "Why are you so eager to die?"

"You've been blackmailing my ma. I'm not going to let you do that."

Slocum thought he was past being surprised at anything. He was wrong.

"What makes you think I'm blackmailing her?"

"You've been nosing around town, asking questions, and you been talking to her. That upsets her every time. This is where it stops."

"You've been doing some digging around town yourself?"

"I found out enough. Draw, Slocum, draw, or I'll cut you down where you stand." Bray's hand shook and moved closer to his pistol.

"All right," Slocum said. His hand was steady and he knew his aim was good, but he didn't want to kill Bray. The young man had followed a trail and found the wrong game at the end. "But I'm not the one you want to call out. I'm working for your pa."

That broke Bray's concentration. For a moment he looked too flustered to do anything. Frozen as he was, he presented the perfect target for Slocum. Two quick steps brought Slocum within range. He swung a haymaker with his left fist and connected with the young man's head, knocking him to the ground. Before he could recover, Slocum snatched the pistol from his holster. Bray lay on the ground stunned. As the shock wore off, it was replaced with towering anger. Slocum knew this couldn't be allowed to stand.

"On your feet. Come on." He grabbed Bray's collar and shoved him along.

"Where you taking me? Not man enough to shoot an unarmed man in front of the whole damned town?"

Slocum didn't bother looking around. He knew people peered out from behind curtains and partly opened doors. They were too smart to come out to watch a gunfight, but they were still intent on the outcome. Slocum shoved Bray along until they came to the bank.

"Inside. Now."

"What are you going to do? Kill my pa, too?"

Slocum kicked the door open with his boot and shoved Bray inside, sending him sprawling. From behind the low wood rail, Martin Bray shot to his feet at his desk.

"What's the meaning of this?"

"You talk to your boy and knock some sense into his head, if you have to. You tell him what I've been doing for you." Slocum tossed Randall Bray's six-gun to his father, who clumsily caught it. "The next time I'll leave him dead in the middle of Main Street."

Slocum left, not bothering to close the door behind him. The tellers were deathly silent as Martin Bray exploded with invective aimed at his son. From what he heard going on inside the bank lobby, Slocum thought Randall Bray was not going to be a fly in the ointment anymore. If he had to, Slocum would tell the bank president where the embezzled money had gone, but he wanted to avoid that for now. Philomena was no prize, but Slocum saw no reason to destroy her marriage or standing in the community when Andrew Molinari was responsible.

He hurried along the boardwalk but slowed when he saw Molinari's two gunmen across the street watching him. His dander was still up, and taking them on here and now suited him just fine. He stepped out into the street, the sun warm at his back.

The two men disappeared as if they were nothing more than smoke. Slocum wasn't sure if he was disappointed. They knew him and had tried to kill him a couple of times. A third time would end with bodies waiting for burial out on Primrose Hill—and Slocum was sure his would not be one of the corpses.

Turning, he went on to Sara Beth's restaurant. The breakfast customers had left and the noontime diners had yet to show up.

"What can I do for you, Mr. Slocum?" Her smile was brighter than the sun outside.

"Coffee."

"That's all? I can offer items not on the menu. To stimulate your appetites."

"Randall Bray tried to get me in a gunfight."

"You kill him?" Sara Beth's smile ran away. "No," she

said, "you didn't. But if you didn't kill him—and I didn't hear any gunshots—that means he's still mad at you."

"He thinks I'm blackmailing his ma." Slocum went on to spell out everything he knew about Molinari and his photography. "He's making good money off Philomena, but she's not the only one. Severigne's girl Missy wants to marry a rancher."

"Hans Lehrer," she said. "News gets around fast in a small town. So this all goes back to photographs Molinari took in Kansas City?"

"He's moved around a lot. He told me he sold pictures of naked women to soldiers during the war. He might still be in that trade. There's no telling how many women he's photographed during his career or where."

"Anna?"

Slocum said, "I don't have proof, and she might just have been a coincidence, but I don't think so. One of Molinari's henchmen killed her and tried to make it look like suicide. I heard his confession, but it would be my word against his in court."

"Emily did kill herself," Sara Beth said, still chewing on that. "But Molinari is responsible."

Slocum held down his anger because he was certain Emily had tried to frame him for her suicide, to make it look like murder, just because he was new in town.

At the black heart of it all stood Molinari with his photographs.

"We need to flush Molinari out," Slocum said.

"Then shoot him out of the air just like you would a quail," Sara Beth finished. "It's only fitting."

"The best way is to work with Missy and her beau," Slocum said. "If Molinari fails with her, maybe everything will come unraveled."

"You are going to have to kill him. Marshal Dunbar isn't likely to arrest him. And one mistake will mean Molinari can show everyone in Wyoming his photographs. How many women would be ruined? How many lives?"

Slocum had to agree.

"Go to Missy and get her to come here," Slocum said. "I'll see if Lehrer can be convinced to talk with her and get this matter straightened out. This is all we can do unless I can lay my hands on the photographic plates."

"Go in with guns blazing, John. Kill him, take them and . . . and smash them!" Sara Beth was flushed from her passion, but Slocum knew it could never be that simple. If he did as she suggested, not even Clabber and Severigne could get him out of jail before he swung from the gallows.

With the power shifting in town, even if Philomena urged her husband to help get him free, Slocum wasn't likely to escape the law. Justice would have nothing to do with it. Dunbar's obvious dislike of him would drive the matter until Slocum got his neck stretched.

"Go get Missy," he said. Sara Beth gave him a quick kiss, but he was distracted, already thinking about how to get Lehrer there.

That proved easier than he'd expected. Simply telling the rancher Missy wanted to talk with him was more than enough to get him back to the restaurant. But when Missy saw him walk in, she shot to her feet and started to run out through the kitchen. If Sara Beth hadn't blocked her way, she would have vanished.

"What's going on?" Lehrer demanded. "I thought you said she wanted to see me. That doesn't look like a woman who wants to meet up with her betrothed."

"We're not gettin' married, Hans. I'm callin' it off. If I didn't make myself clear last night, I am now. Leave me alone." Missy broke into tears.

"You want to tell him about last night and who you met?" Slocum asked.

Missy turned whiter than a bleached muslin sheet. She shook her head and then recovered her wits. She grabbed Slocum by the arm and dragged him to the corner of the dining room.

"You know everything?"

"I saw Molinari try to blackmail you. Looks like he's succeeding, too. There can't be anything in that picture he showed you that Lehrer doesn't know about."

Missy turned even whiter. Her lips thinned to a razor slash, and she stabbed her index finger into Slocum's chest so hard he took a step back.

"You listen up good, Slocum. You don't know anything about that photograph, and I never want Hans to either. Ever."

"He knows what you do for a living, and he wants to marry you. That tells me he's a man who knows what he wants and isn't going to stop till he gets it."

"Well, he ain't gettin' me!" Tears welled in her eyes again. She spun and shouted at Lehrer, "You get on back to your ranch. I don't ever want to see you again."

She bolted past Slocum and got outside. He followed her and stopped her.

"Don't you love Lehrer?"

"With all my heart, and that's why I ain't seein' him hurt. Or seein' how his love for me would dissolve like a sugar lump in vinegar."

"Did Molinari tell you not to marry Lehrer?" Slocum had some crazy idea the photographer wanted Missy for himself. That notion died in a flash.

"He *ordered* me to marry Hans." Missy broke free and ran off, sobbing as she went. Slocum stared after her, aware of how people up and down Main Street were staring at him. It had been his day to draw unwanted attention to himself. He went back inside, where Sara Beth tried to calm Lehrer. She wasn't getting too far.

"What got into that woman, Slocum? Severigne said you'd make sure everything went smooth. It's been just the opposite."

"If me butting out would help matters, I would," Slocum said. "There's someone dealing himself into this game who doesn't belong."

"I told him, John. I told him Molinari had pictures."

"And I don't care. I saw what that photographer did for Severigne to advertise her whorehouse. They're right good pictures, and the one of Missy's fine enough for me to frame and put up—out of the front room, of course. Back where just we could see it. But that's nothing for her to be ashamed over."

"I'll deal with Molinari," Slocum said. "Don't you go near him, and watch out for his two hired gunmen. They're a pair of back shooters, for certain sure."

"I'm not afraid of the photographer or his hired guns or the Devil himself if it means I can be with Missy."

Slocum almost told Lehrer that Molinari wanted the marriage to proceed so that he could siphon every cent he could out of the H Bar L Ranch and its owner's new wife. He held back because he had heard and believed what both Missy and Lehrer said. Whatever was in the photograph was worse than a nude pose.

"You do that, Slocum. Don't take too long or I'll tend to this myself."

"Try and Missy might run where you'll never find her."

Lehrer snorted.

"I can track real good. I'll carry a kerosene lamp through the bowels of hell to find her, if that's what it takes." Lehrer stomped out of the restaurant, leaving an uncomfortable silence in his wake.

"What now, John?" Sara Beth finally asked.

"Time to take the bull by the horns." He touched his six-shooter and then took his hand away, not wanting to give Sara Beth any ideas about what he intended. There might be lead flying, but he wanted to settle this quick. If Molinari died, Marshal Dunbar would never rest until he had somebody locked up in jail for it. The first person he'd come after would be John Slocum.

"I want to come with you." She clutched his arm. "If what you said about Emily is true, it was Molinari who drove her to such desperation."

"You've got a customer," Slocum said. As Sara Beth

turned toward the hungry cowboy, he was out the back way in a flash. He never slowed as he headed for Molinari's office. Plans formed and died in seconds. There wasn't any reason to be subtle about it.

Slocum stopped in front of the office, then drew his six-gun and kicked in the door. The hasp and lock ripped from the wood and the hinges sagged from the impact of his boot. Slocum stepped into the room. The empty room. He ought to have known Molinari wasn't inside since there had been a lock on the door. He swung around, to be sure Molinari wasn't hiding behind the curtains and other backdrops he used for his photographs.

The family photos. The ones everyone in town thought were his bread and butter. Using his heel, Slocum kicked shut the door and holstered his pistol. He had a search ahead of him.

He went directly to Molinari's desk, where he had found the strongbox before, but it was gone. Slocum cursed under his breath, but this was to be expected. The photographer would move his blackmail pictures somewhere harder to find. Ignoring the obvious places, Slocum looked for loose floorboards or secret doors in furniture where a packet of photographs might be hidden.

After fifteen minutes he hadn't found anything. Molinari could well have taken the box and hidden it elsewhere.

Slocum sat in the man's chair and looked around. If he were Molinari, he would keep the blackmail photographs somewhere that he could watch. The prospect of Molinari hiding the incriminating pictures outside this office meant Slocum had no chance at all of ever finding them, short of Molinari taking him to them.

"They must be here. He's such an arrogant bastard, he'd want them close at hand and not think anybody would find them."

Slocum slowly scanned the room and couldn't find a single place in the almost-bare studio where a strongbox could be hidden. That was probably why Molinari had kept it in the knee well of his desk. It was close there, and out of sight.

As Slocum stood to begin a new search, the door to the office opened. All he saw was the rifle barrel and not the gunman behind the weapon.

The muzzle belched orange flame and smoke. The bullet tore past Slocum and dug a hole in the chair where he had been sitting. He drew and fired, but the slug tore into the door rather than the gunman. Diving, Slocum skidded across the room and came to a halt behind a stack of crates. His nose wrinkled at the pungent smell. These were Molinari's chemicals used in developing the pictures.

The rifleman pushed open the door using the barrel, then figured out where Slocum hid. Using the doorjamb for cover, he began firing as fast as he could lever in a new round.

The lead tore past Slocum and then began hitting the crates in front of him. He waited until seven shots were fired in his direction, then poked up over the top of the crates and began firing. The gunman changed to his handgun, forcing Slocum back.

As the man peeked around the door, Slocum saw it was one of Molinari's henchmen.

"You come on out and I won't shoot you down like a mad dog," the gunman called. Slocum heard him reloading his rifle and knew what his fate would be if he tried to surrender.

But he worried that he might have to. The fumes rising from in front of the pile of crates burned his eyes and made breathing difficult. Too many rifle bullets had ripped into the crates and shattered glass bottles that now dripped out their noxious contents. He coughed and finally pulled up his bandanna to protect his nose and mouth. That helped his breathing but did nothing for his increasingly watery eyes.

Slocum got off a couple more shots as he wondered what to do. His boot soles were starting to sizzle and burn as the liquid from the crates pooled around his feet.

"All right, I'm coming out," Slocum called, waiting to see what response he got.

"Throw out your gun, then come on out with your hands high."

Slocum stood, grabbed the top crate, and heaved as hard as he could. It crashed to the floor just inside the door. Molinari's henchman reacted instinctively and fired several times. Slocum rushed the door, firing as he came. He slipped in a pool of chemical and lurched forward. The last round in his Colt Navy flew straight and true, in spite of the situation. As he fell, going to his knees and one hand, he saw that his slug had ripped a bloody chunk out of the man's gun arm.

The gunman grabbed his injured right biceps as the rifle slipped from nerveless fingers. He snarled at Slocum, turned, and sprinted off, spewing blood as he ran.

Slocum lifted his pistol, got him in the sights, and dry-fired. The hammer fell on a spent chamber. He groaned as he got to his feet, his jeans burning away from the chemicals.

By now a dozen people down the street shouted for the marshal. Slocum considered going after the wounded gunman, then decided against it. He was never one to let wounded game go into the woods to suffer, but this was different. He wanted the man to feel pain for a good long while because of what he'd done to Anna—and then he would get him in his sights again and finish the job he'd just started.

Slocum stumbled off, his denim jeans with holes burned in them and his boots splotchy from the potent chemicals. At least he could breathe fresh air again—and was still in good enough shape to keep breathing.

That was a condition he vowed to change for Molinari and his murderous hired guns.

17

Slocum limped to the watering trough near Severigne's barn. He shucked off his six-shooter and gun belt, then sat on the edge of the trough, wondering if this would work.

"To hell with it," he said. His skin was blistered and burned from the chemicals that had splashed onto his jeans and boots. Swiveling around, he shoved his feet under water and recoiled as huge bubbles burst on the surface. He dropped to his knees in the trough to get his pant legs entirely underwater. A sudden sharp pain passed quickly, replaced by soothing coolness. Sighing, he stretched out and sat on the bottom of the trough, arms on the sides. He had no idea how long he ought to stay, but he knew he had to empty the trough after he got out. This water wasn't fit for any animal to drink anymore.

After five minutes, he stood and looked at his ruined jeans. His boots were in better condition since the acid had so much heavier leather to burn through. He began skinning off his pants when he heard a loud wolf whistle. Alice stood at the barn door, leering at him.

"I wondered what it would take to get into your pants," she said. "I never thought about the watering trough."

He held up the pants. Sunlight shone through the holes. "There a spare pair somewhere that I can borrow?"

"Might be," Alice said. "For a price." He glared at her and she relented. "Oh, very well. There's an old pair in the barn. I don't remember who left them, but he was in a hurry. I think his missus tracked him here."

She went into the barn and came out with a pair of jeans even more battered than the ones with the acid holes burned in them. Slocum took them and found that the former owner was thicker around the waist. He had to cinch up his belt to keep them from falling down. This produced snickers from Alice.

"Sometime you'll have to tell me what happened." She held up his old pants and started to run her finger around a hole.

"Don't. You might get burned. I don't know how long it'd take for the water to wash it all away."

"You are the most fascinating man to come to Severigne's in a month of Sundays. Maybe ever." Alice looked at him appraisingly. "Too bad I got me a steady gentleman friend."

Slocum thought on how she could whore all night but consider the bank teller a boyfriend. Every profession was different.

"How did Bray deal with his son?"

"After you tossed him into the bank lobby?" Alice laughed and it sounded genuine. "You made quite an impression on young Randall, but his old man made a permanent one. He used his belt on his son's bottom."

"Randall's eighteen or thereabouts. That could be dangerous for his pa."

"Randall's not got hair on his balls yet, no matter how he comes sniffing around here all the time. And you were right. It was him what tried to set fire to the house. That got him another swat or two from the belt. It didn't sound as if there wasn't anything he didn't confess to. If Martin had kept whalin' on him much longer, Randall might even have confessed to assassinating Lincoln."

If Randall Bray had a speck of gumption in him, he would be ten times more dangerous. As if he wasn't doing so already, Slocum would have to watch his back to keep from getting shot down. For being a newcomer to town, he had piled up enemies at an incredible rate.

"What is it you're doing for Bray? He said you were working for him." Alice came closer, intent on hearing the answer.

"Ask Severigne. If she wants to tell you, she will."

"That's downright mysterious. As I said, you're the most interesting fellow to come by in years."

"I need to talk with her. Is she inside?"

"Gone. Not sure where, but she had that look in her eye, if you know what I mean."

"Business or pleasure?"

"No reason it can't be both. Severigne's always on the lookout for customers, but she's not above mixing the two."

"Where does she keep the catalog?"

"The one the photographer put together as advertising? I'm not sure."

Slocum wanted to look it over carefully to see if there might be some clue as to where Molinari would hide the other pictures. Then he decided that was only a waste of time. Why should there be any? The photographer wouldn't put clues like that into a new catalog.

"Did he keep photographs for his own collection?"

"I assumed that he did. He was a gentleman taking the pictures, but he has the plates to make as many copies as he wants. Severigne wanted to buy them but he refused."

"I suspected as much." If any of the girls working for Severigne tried to leave their lives as whores, Molinari would have blackmail material to hold over them with their husbands. Somehow, Slocum doubted many of the remaining women would be all that susceptible to blackmail. Alice certainly wouldn't be, though Catherine was with her ranch foreman. And Missy's marriage to a successful rancher had been derailed, though Slocum was still at a loss to figure out how bad the photograph might be since Lehrer seemed a reasonable hombre about her current profession.

"There's a whole lot going on I don't know about," Alice said. "What would it take for me to get you to tell me all the sordid details?"

"More than time or your bed."

"Well," Alice said, insulted. Or at least she pretended to be insulted. "After I got you another pair of pants. See if I do that again when I find you sitting in a trough with your old pair turned into nothing but holes."

"Much obliged for the jeans," Slocum said. He mounted and rode back into town, Alice calling after him until he was out of earshot. He liked her and wished her and her teller the best. But he doubted the teller had much of a future at the bank considering Alice's situation. Bray would never allow an employee to marry a soiled dove, which was ironic considering he had unwittingly done that very thing himself.

He dismounted in front of Sara Beth's restaurant, took in the commotion inside, then drew his pistol and shoved his way through the crowd, yelling, "What's going on?"

"It's Miz Vincent," a man said. "She took sick. She was fine one minute, then she was all wobbly in the knees and keeled over. They done took her to the doctor."

"They?" Slocum looked around at the sea of faces.

"I think the two of 'em work for Mr. Molinari. I seen 'em there a time or two. One of them was all busted up himself. Had his right arm in a sling, like he'd broke his arm."

"Tell me exactly what happened," Slocum said. The man looked frightened, and Slocum realized he was pointing his six-shooter directly at him. He holstered it and pulled a chair around. The crowd seemed to grow. This was the most excitement they'd had since gunshots were fired at Molinari's office earlier. Slocum was quickly running out of patience for such "excitement."

"Well, she was bringin' me a platter of that meatloaf she does so good. Taters on the side and—" The man swallowed hard when he saw Slocum's expression. "Well, she put it down and wiped her lips with her apron and then got all white in the face. I had her set down right where you're settin' and ast what was wrong and if she needed a drink of water. She said she'd just had one in the back and was feeling all weak and dizzy. 'Bout then them two fellers barged in and took her out, sayin' they was right away takin' her to the doc's office."

Slocum went to the kitchen, where he found the water bucket on the table. He sniffed hard at it and recoiled from the strong odor. He had smelled this too many times before in saloons when the barkeep wanted to get rid of an obnoxious customer. A drop or two of chloral hydrate would fell an ox. From the strong smell, somebody had put more than a few drops into the water, knowing Sara Beth would drink it.

He knew exactly who it was, too.

When he returned to the dining room, most of the crowd had left. The man with the plate of meatloaf in front of him was polishing off the last bit of gravy with a hunk of bread. He licked his lips clean as he looked up at Slocum.

"She be all right, you think? Miz Vincent's a right good cook and easy on the eyes."

Slocum knew where the doctor's office was from his prior nighttime visit, but it was as he figured. The two owlhoots had not taken Sara Beth there. The doctor claimed not to have seen Sara Beth since breakfast, and Slocum believed him.

His mind raced as to why Molinari would kidnap Sara Beth. If he thought she was a nuisance and likely to get in his way, why not kill her? Ransom was the most likely explanation, but Slocum couldn't come up with two nickels to rub together. Severigne wasn't inclined to pony up money, even if Slocum asked her to. Clyde Clabber? Martin Bray? The banker was already being fleeced out of every last cent in his bank and didn't know how it was happening. Molinari would want to cast his net farther afield than the banker if he wanted more money.

Why had he drugged and taken Sara Beth prisoner?

The only explanation he could come up with was to use her as a bargaining chip. Slocum had been poking about in Molinari's blackmail scheme too much and hadn't been eliminated after repeated attempts. He must have been thinking to trade Sara Beth for Slocum moving on—or maybe getting put in a grave out on Primrose Hill. Molinari would ask for an exchange and then gun down both Sara Beth and Slocum at the same time. The marshal wasn't likely to investigate, especially if Molinari got rid of the bodies where nobody would ever find them. This part of Wyoming was mighty lonely once you rode away from town.

Slocum wondered how Molinari intended to get in touch to present his bogus offer. Probably a letter would be sent to Severigne. Slocum intended to find Sara Beth before that note could be delivered.

He went up one side and down the other along Main Street, asking which way the two men had taken Sara Beth. He finally gathered enough information to get on the road going due east out onto the prairie. Hans Lehrer's spread was in that direction, but he doubted Molinari's men would go there. They had no call to involve the rancher.

Slocum felt a grim satisfaction knowing that Molinari thought he was a more immediate risk than Missy refusing to marry the rancher. After he was out of the way, Molinari would apply more pressure on the woman to force her to marry Lehrer and begin yet another stream of blackmail money.

As he rode, he scanned the prairie all around for any trace of the outlaws or where they might have taken Sara Beth. He doubted they would go far from town so when he saw a deep ravine cutting toward the southeast, he paid special attention to where it crossed the main road. He smiled without humor when he saw fresh tracks leaving the road and heading down the bottom of the ravine. The high sides would hide the riders from casual observation and the ravine must lead somewhere that the men felt was safe.

Two miles brought him to a flat area where spring runoff scrubbed the land clean and left nothing but ripples in the earth. Off a ways from this fan-shaped stretch rose a shack, hardly more than a lean-to. Even at this distance Slocum made out horses tethered to one side. Three horses. Just the right number for the two gunmen and Sara Beth.

He took out his field glasses and studied the area surrounding the cabin. It was too flat for him to sneak up on the shack unless they hadn't bothered posting a lookout. Slocum held down his rage when he realized they probably weren't expecting pursuit—and that they would be occupied with Sara Beth. The thought of her being raped by the pair caused him to feel a coldness that reminded him of the days during the war when he had been a sniper. He would spend hours waiting for just the right shot at a Federal officer. It had never paid to get excited or anticipate the shot since he never knew when opportunity would present itself.

The calmness was always cold and calculating and utterly deadly. That was what he experienced now.

He dismounted and took his Winchester from the saddle sheath. He tied his horse's reins around a rock and then started walking toward the shack, eyes hunting for the slightest movement. It would take him only an instant to bring the rifle to his shoulder for the killing shot.

He got all the way to the shed before the horses even bothered to whinny and paw uneasily at the ground. Their small noises wouldn't draw attention from the men inside, not if they were consumed with Sara Beth.

The cabin didn't have any windows for him to peek through so he went directly to the door and pressed his face against it, trying to see inside through a crack. A sudden brilliance caused him to jerk back. His right eye was dazzled from the light, momentarily blinding him. From inside came raucous laughter.

"That oughta be one to keep."

"Molinari will like it, that's for sure. How many more we got to take?"

"Three," came the answer.

In spite of the yellow and blue spots dancing in front of Slocum's right eye, he kicked in the door and leveled the rifle, not knowing what to expect. The men stood behind a camera and Sara Beth was tied up, naked, to a post in a lewd position.

They were taking blackmail pictures of her.

Slocum fired.

The light blazed again from the T-shaped contraption in one man's hand. Slocum was completely blinded this time. He levered in another round and fired, knowing he might hit Sara Beth and not caring. It might be better if she was killed rather than suffer the indignity of having those blackmail photos shown around Clabber Crossing.

He fired a third time and was rewarded by a grunt. Then he was bowled over, knocked backward, and the rifle was yanked from his grip. Slocum landed hard on his back. Looking out of the corner of his eye, he saw a man with his arm in a sling holding the rifle clumsily in his left hand. Slocum kicked out and smashed his boot into the man's kneecap.

"He busted my damn leg!" came the cry. The man vanished from the corner of Slocum's eye, but the dancing yellow and blue specks were fading. He saw Molinari's other henchman come from the shed, a six-gun in his grip.

Slocum reached across his body, pulled his own pistol, and fired.

Then he yelled, "Marshal, over here. I got 'em. Both of 'em!"

"Son of a bitch, he musta brung a posse." The one in the

doorway ducked, helped his partner up, and they made their way around the side of the shed. Slocum fired a couple more times and kept yelling for the marshal to come.

Hooves pounding into the distance gave him the chance to sink back to the ground. Where the man had struck him in the chest hurt like fire. Slocum gently probed to see if he might have a broken rib. The pain was different from a broken bone; he was only bruised. He sat up, then got to his feet. By now his vision was returning.

He looked into the shed where the camera was pointed at Sara Beth. She was bound with her hands over her head. She was bent at a crazy angle so her legs were spread wide. From this direction, they got a lewd photograph of her not only tied up but of her privates.

"Are you going to stand there gawking or are you going to get me free?" she demanded.

Slocum started to josh her a bit and then decided against it. He cut her free and she collapsed into his arms, sobbing.

18

Slocum held the shaking woman as he took a quick look around the interior of the shack. Molinari's hired guns had been taking photographs. Sitting beside the camera, apparently ready for another shot, stood a wooden case where the exposed plates were stored.

"They kept talking about shooting a dozen of them. I don't know why they wanted a dozen, but they did. They posed me in terrible ways."

"They do anything but take pictures?" Slocum asked. Sara Beth shuddered in his arms.

"They said they would later—and they'd take pictures of that, too. John, I could never hold my head up again if they showed those photographs around town."

"You'd have done anything they wanted," he said.

She buried her face in his shoulder and sobbed. Molinari would have owned Sara Beth Vincent with an album of these pictures. The power in Clabber Crossing was slowly shifting, and neither the town's founder nor the town banker knew it. Their squabbles were petty compared to the power Molinari was gaining over the women in town. And who could the women complain to? Where could they turn for justice?

"Get dressed. It won't be long before those two sons of bitches figure out I didn't have a posse at my back."

"You lied?"

"A diversionary tactic," he said, reaching down to heft the case. Special baffles had been built so an exposed plate could be slipped inside for later developing.

"That's what they did with the plates," Sara Beth said, getting into her clothing. She misbuttoned her blouse and her skirt was askew, but Slocum wasn't going to mention it. There were more important things to tend to first. He carried the case outside into the bright sun.

"Light ruins the image," he said, opening the latches and pulling away the black cloth coverings inside. He laid out all of the plates so the full rays of the sun struck them. He stepped back and looked at the glass plates, then began stomping on them. One by one he crushed the plates until the glass blended in with the sandy soil. "That ought to take care of the problem," he said.

"You didn't save just one plate?" Sara Beth asked.

"None. Why?"

"Oh, it might have looked good hanging on the wall of the restaurant."

He saw that her sense of humor was coming back.

"You wouldn't have dared," he said. Before she could protest, he went on. "You'd have too many customers to feed. Every meal, the men in Clabber Crossing would be lined up waiting to get inside just to look at the pretty picture of the pretty owner."

"Well, the business would have been nice," she said, as if thinking it over, "but I suppose I'll have to depend on good cooking instead."

She mounted and was ready to go, but Slocum wanted to finish the job he had started. The photographic plates were destroyed, leaving all the equipment in the shack untouched. He fumbled in his vest pocket and pulled out the tin holding his lucifers. He fished one out, struck it on his left cuff, and then tossed the flaming match into the ramshackle building. A couple seconds later a gout of flame erupted from the door, then the roof collapsed. With the extra fuel, the fire turned the shack into a fiery furnace that would burn itself out when the camera equipment had long since turned to cinders and melted glass.

Slocum stepped up into the saddle and looked across the prairie in the direction taken by the two owlhoots as they escaped. Tracking them down would be a pleasure, but Slocum had Sara Beth to think about.

"Back to town?" she asked.

"Not directly, in case they cut back at an angle and get between us and Clabber Crossing along the road." He pointed due north and they set off riding at a canter. In the hot sun Slocum didn't want to tire their horses but had to get the hell away from this spot if Molinari's men returned.

"Where are we headed?"

"Someplace they won't find us," Slocum said. He doubled back on the trail a couple times, then started getting inventive about hiding their tracks. Dragging a wad of weeds behind wasn't much use since the prairie was deathly still. The drag marks would stand out more than the hoofprints in the hard ground. If the wind had been kicking up, he would have tried that since the drag marks might have been mistaken for wind ridges. Even better, the loosened dirt would have been blown all over their tracks.

As it was, the best way of getting away from pursuit was to make good time away, and by sundown he knew they had escaped. A cabin ahead looked promising and he rode up to it.

"Hello? Anybody home?"

"Deserted," Sara Beth said. "From the look of the land around here, a sodbuster tried to grow wheat or corn and didn't make it. Ranching is a better way of making a living out here, and for that you need a lot of rangeland, not a dinky little plot like this."

The cabin had the air of being long deserted. Slocum dismounted and warily poked his head inside, then signaled to Sara Beth to join him. It was mostly empty, though a crude bed remained, its rope supports rotted through by time and weather. The wind would have whipped through the chinks in the walls and turned this into an icy coffin in winter.

"We're not sleeping on that," she said, running her fingers over a strand. The rope turned to dust at her light touch.

"Won't matter," Slocum said, scraping away debris to clear a spot on the dirt floor. "That's too small for two."

"Oh? And what did you have in mind? Something horribly salacious," Sara Beth said, turning to him.

"You'll have to show me what that means."

"All right!" And she fell into his arms. "You saved me, John," she said in a husky voice. "You saved me from a life of slavery to that horrid man."

He silenced her with a kiss. Or did she keep him from answering? It didn't matter. They moved slowly around and around, exploring with their mouths, letting their hands tug and pull and open to get rid of unwanted clothing.

He finally pulled her blouse back and buried his face between her breasts. She shivered in delight at the feel of his tongue moving in the deep valley, up the slopes, and across the sensitive nubs. Then it was her turn. Sara Beth kissed his bare chest, tangled wetly in the hair she found with her tongue, and worked lower until she pulled his manhood from his battered jeans. She engulfed the knobby end and sucked hard.

Slocum caught his breath as sensation built within him. Her tongue played about the underside, all over the tip, until tingles grew within and lightning threatened to flash. He pushed her away. The blonde rocked back on her heels, a motion that caused her breasts to gently bob in the most beguiling manner possible.

He sank down in front of her on the blanket he had spread on the floor. He moved forward—she moved backward. He followed as she sank slowly to the blanket and made wiggling motions with her hips.

"Floor's uneven," she said.

She cried out as he reached around her, lifted her bodily, and shifted around before lowering her gently again.

"That better?"

"No," she said. She reached down and caught at his rigid length, tugging it toward her. She pulled up her skirt and guided him directly to her nether lips. "Now. This is better." She arched her back and crammed herself down around him.

Slocum shoved forward at the same instant and buried himself balls deep within her. For a moment they clung to one another like that, merged and more. Then he began moving, slowly at first and with increasing need, increasing speed until friction burned away at him. Sara Beth writhed beneath him and clutched hard at his arms. She threw her arms around his neck and pulled him down.

He had wanted to look into her lovely face and watch the passion grow but she wanted more. He kissed her lips. Moving about, he nibbled at her ear and then worked down to kiss the arch of her throat. All the while he continued to thrust forward at a steady pace that soon became impossible to maintain.

Urgency grew in him. White-hot fire burned and then exploded outward as he made love to her. And then she cried out, dug her fingernails into his bare back, and sagged to the floor. She was sweating but the glow on her face came from within, not from the sunlight slanting in through a crack in the wall and turning her perspiration to tiny, shining diamonds.

Pressed together in the afternoon heat, they said nothing because there was no need. Finally, Slocum rolled away and stood.

"You're quite a sight from this angle," Sara Beth said, looking up at him. She licked her lips and looked feral and wild.

"Hungry?"

"For me?"

"Later," Slocum said. "You wore me out."

"You need more practice," she said. "Not that I'm complaining, but a girl's got to make sure her man can keep up with her."

Slocum laughed, knelt, and kissed her.

"I'm hungry for food. I'm surprised you're not, too."

"Well, I am. I miss being in the kitchen. I love fixing all that food, even if I'm not the one going to eat it. I sample everything, though," she said. She lounged back, put her hands behind her head, and stretched. The way she arched her back presented her bare bosom to him again.

But Slocum wasn't going to be enticed again, not yet. He dressed and stepped out to look around the prairie. To the west lay Clabber Crossing and farther beyond the town rose the majestic, purple-swathed Grand Tetons. This was beautiful country, and Sara Beth was a beautiful woman. He half turned when she came up behind him and wrapped her arms around his waist. She laid her cheek against his back.

"We have to return to town, don't we?"

"Eventually. In the morning," he said.

"I wish this could last forever, just the two of us out here, alone."

Slocum didn't answer. He had been thinking the same thing until he saw the mountains rising in the distance and had wondered, fleetingly, what lay beyond them. That tug was even stronger on him than any invisible bonds Sara Beth might use to hog-tie him.

They ate, went back into the cabin, and spent a night together filled with passion and a sense of distance. By midday they rode back into Clabber Crossing.

Sara Beth waved and smiled brightly at the people along the street. Some turned to whisper to friends but most returned the greeting.

"Your reputation is going to be dragged through the mud, riding into town with me like this."

"What do I care what they think?"

"You have to live with them."

"So do you," she said, her eyes going straight forward. Her shoulders slumped.

"I work as a bouncer in a whorehouse because I lost a poker hand to the town's founder. That's all they'll ever think of me."

"But you're doing the marshal's work for him. You—you saved me from kidnappers. From Molinari."

"I intend to save the reputations of other women, but I need to destroy everything in that strongbox that was in Molinari's office." Slocum kicked himself for not destroying it when he had the chance. Now the photographer would have hidden it where no one would ever find it.

"He must have the box where the contents can be passed out if anything happens to him. He'd think of it as a life insurance policy. Kill him, and the photographs are made public."

"He might have told his partners, but I don't think so. They aren't any more than hired gunmen." Slocum laughed harshly as the thought came to him that Molinari might have put the box into Bray's bank. The banker might be safeguarding the very evidence that was causing his wife to steal from him.

"A lawyer?" Sara Beth suggested. "We've got a couple in town, but they are pretty much in the hip pockets of Clabber and Bray. Either one of them would turn over anything put in his custody if their real bosses asked."

"He might be working the same blackmail racket with other photographers. Who knows? He might have copied it from somebody he worked for back in Kansas City."

"You're saying he hid the photographs and somebody else will know where to find them if Molinari is killed?"

"It makes sense. He could send a letter to another photographer, who would retrieve the strongbox and pick up where Molinari left off. Why let such good blackmail evidence go to waste?"

Sara Beth shivered in spite of the heat. She turned and looked at Slocum for a moment before saying, "You're going to have to kill him. No matter what, John. If you don't, I will!"

"It's not your reputation at stake since he doesn't have pictures of you."

"You stopped those two in time. But even if it means the reason for Emily's death is revealed, it has to be done. Secrecy is what makes his hold so powerful."

"You'll ruin others along the way," Slocum said. He thought of Philomena Bray and Catherine, out west of town getting ready to marry her ranch foreman. And whatever Molinari had said to Missy kept her from marrying her rancher. That was likely to cause an explosion nobody liked. If Slocum read Hans Lehrer right, the man wasn't inclined to take no for an answer and had left Texas because of it.

"What are you going to do? Can you force Molinari to tell you where he hid the photographs?"

"I don't think so." Slocum sized up men well and didn't think Molinari would break, no matter what he did. The man would take too much delight knowing that, once dead, his vile legacy would continue to poison the lives of countless women. Slocum knew that only those women who had somehow come to Clabber Crossing had fallen under the photographer's thumb.

Before Slocum could say more, he saw sudden movement from the corner of his eye. His hand went to his six-shooter, but he stopped when he saw the preacher's boy dash away. Edgar Dawson had watched as they rode past, hidden behind a rain barrel.

"I have an idea. Nothing may come of it, but it's worth following up." He left Sara Beth shouting at him to explain. Putting his head down, he urged his horse to a full gallop after Edgar. He rode down an alley to a secondary street. Whoever had laid out the town had done it along the main road with only a few parallel streets. He rapidly passed those and found himself going south of town where the terrain made building more difficult. A few houses perched on the hillsides but mostly the area was undeveloped. Slowing, he strained every sense to find the boy.

A rustle of leaves to his right brought him around. He didn't see Edgar, but the way the bushes shuddered didn't match the slight breeze blowing. Trotting over, he saw a scrap of cloth caught on an inch-long thorn. Although he had gotten only a quick look at the boy, he thought this matched his shirt. Slocum dismounted and began tracking on foot. A half hour later he had circled most of the town and had come back to a spot between the church and the Dawson house.

The ground was too hard for decent tracking, but Slocum thought he knew where Edgar had gone to ground. Approaching the shack where Emily Dawson had taken her own life, Slocum saw signs someone had been inside recently. He tethered his horse and looked around inside the shack, then smiled. The boy wouldn't have his secret hideout here. Outside, Slocum looked around the area for a tall enough tree with leaves hiding the trunk high up. He walked to a battered tree where lightning had knocked down a huge limb, affording a way up to the trunk that was better than any ladder. He saw fresh smears in the sap.

Digging his toes into the wood, he made his way to the trunk, caught another limb, and pulled himself up so he could block Edgar's escape unless the boy wanted to risk a fifteen-foot drop to the ground.

"Go away."

Slocum shook his head and settled down.

"I want it."

"No."

From the boy's frightened expression Slocum knew he had hit pay dirt. He settled back, leaning against the trunk, and waited Edgar out.

"You won't tell?"

"I won't tell anyone. But I need the photographs."

"You'll let me keep one or two?"

"Nope," Slocum said. "They aren't yours, and Molinari is using them to hurt people."

"People? There's only one lady in the pictures, and she's mighty pretty. Kinda blurred, but . . ."

Slocum caught his breath. How could he have been wrong about the contents of the strongbox? He knew Philomena's photograph was in there since he had seen it. He couldn't understand why Molinari would keep only hers in the strongbox.

"Show me," Slocum said.

"There. Behind you. Up higher." Edgar pointed. Slocum craned his neck around and saw a hollow in the tree trunk. Aware that this might be a ploy to escape, Slocum carefully stood and reached around in the nook. His fingers closed on a book. Pulling it out, he frowned. This was a slender album, similar to the one Molinari had given Severigne with the photographs of all her girls.

He dropped back down to the limb and opened the book. Slocum looked up when he saw the half-naked woman in the pictures.

"There are eleven there," Edgar said. "One was missing when I, uh, borrowed the book. I don't know what happened to the photograph but the ones left are . . ." The boy's voice trailed off.

Slocum leafed through the album quickly and saw all were of one woman—Edgar's mother.

"Who is she? The woman in the pictures?" Slocum asked.

Edgar shrugged. He fumbled in his pocket and took out a piece of peppermint candy, looked at it as if thinking about offering it to Slocum, then popped it into his mouth. Only after he had it settled between cheek and teeth did he say anything more.

"I couldn't make out her face so much but, well, that

wasn't what I looked at. You didn't lie, did you? You're not gonna get me in trouble, are you?"

"You're sure you don't know who this is?"

"No. Who is it? Somebody you know?"

Slocum stared at Edgar Dawson for any sign the boy was lying. There wasn't any sign that he knew this was his mother in the photographs. Slocum thought that Molinari had taken one photograph from the album and used that to set Emily on the road to suicide. Edgar had stolen the photo album after Molinari had begun blackmailing his mother.

"Was this the only album?" Slocum asked.

The boy looked away, as if considering how hard he'd land if he jumped to the ground. He squirmed for a minute, then shook his head.

"Did you take the others?"

"I'm gonna get into trouble," Edgar said.

"Not if I get the rest."

"I shouldn't peek in windows, but I like it. I like seeing the ladies' bare skin. My pa says that's a sin and I'll burn in hell."

"That's between you and God. This is here and now," Slocum said. "Might be you could erase some of that spying if you help me."

"That's all I got. I didn't take any others."

"You stop looking through windows or you'll be sure to get into big trouble."

"You gonna tell my pa?"

"I said I wouldn't, but you might tell him yourself. He might tan your hide good, but knowing your pa, he might not."

"I don't like it when he shuns me. That ain't what he calls it, but he won't talk to me and—"

"That's up to you. He and your ma taught you good enough to know what's right and what's wrong." Slocum tucked the album into his belt, swung around, and shinnied down the tree, dropping the last five feet. He took the impact by bending his knees, then looked up at Edgar. The boy sat staring at him, tears running down his cheeks. Edgar started to say something, then looked away.

Slocum let him stew in his own juices. He had his own battle to fight, and the album would go a ways toward winning it.

19

"So you think this will end it?" Severigne asked. She stared hard at Slocum, as if she thought he was lying.

"I can't say, but it'll go a ways toward keeping him from doing this to any more women," Slocum said.

"Why do you care? They are whores. Nothing to you. They sell themselves for the pleasure of men like you."

"I've partaken of the charms of a soiled dove or two in my day," Slocum said, "and I've seen how hard it is. This place is paradise compared to some whorehouses I've seen." Slocum tapped the album with Emily Dawson's pictures. "She was mighty young in this picture. What drove her to such a place in her life that she let Molinari shoot the pictures?"

"Why do you care?"

"I care," Slocum said, "because it's not right for anyone to do what Molinari is doing. He's ruining lives."

"You are sure Emily killed herself because of the missing picture?"

"No," Slocum admitted, "but it fits the facts. He showed her the picture when he got into town from traveling around the countryside and saw the new preacher's wife. She couldn't bear the notion of what having her past exposed would do to her husband and son."

"Death was preferable?" Severigne scoffed, but Slocum saw she was agreeing this was an honorable thing to do. Sacrifice for family outweighed life. "How could she know he would not still reveal the pictures?"

"She didn't, but she finally got lucky. Edgar stole the album and Molinari didn't have any more photographs of her."

"But the plates?"

"They're heavy. He might have left them in Kansas City or sold them or maybe he didn't even take the pictures." Slocum explained how other photographers might have worked the blackmail scheme, swapping photographs, and how he thought Molinari left instructions with another photographer where he had hidden his stash of blackmail photos.

"So killing him is not good?"

"Didn't say that, but at least three women's reputations stand to be ruined if I cut him down like a mad dog and their pictures are spread around."

"You do not know what these photos are?"

"Or where they are."

"Find out. Arrange for this whole sordid matter to go away and you are free of your debt to me. More. I will pay you for those photos."

Slocum wasn't going to promise that. But he did say, "If I disappear or get shot down, make sure the marshal knows. Keep his feet to the fire."

"Pah!" Severigne said dismissively. "I will come for Molinari myself. The law is no good if it allows such as this!"

"Then tell Clabber or Bray—tell both men. Let them decide how to get even with Molinari."

"That might work. Clabber values the reputation of the town that carries his name, and Bray wants to own it. He would be forever disgraced if Philomena's pictures were made public."

"Don't tell him about his wife," Slocum said sharply.

"He doesn't need to know more about her past than he thinks he knows now."

"Go. Do what you must."

Slocum picked up the album, but Severigne grabbed for it. He kept it from her.

"I need this to get Molinari's attention. He knows it's missing. He probably was bluffing after sending Emily the first picture about showing the rest. This will shake him up, and maybe he'll make a mistake."

"Go to his hiding place, eh?" Severigne rocked her head back and forth. "It is what you call a long shot. Good luck, Slocum."

The way Severigne said that, Slocum knew she didn't expect him to return. As he left through the kitchen, he saw Alice watching him. He had never seen her look so grave. She smiled wanly and blew him a kiss, then hurried up the back stairs. Her clicking footsteps died out, and Slocum felt suddenly alone. But he knew what he had to do. Clutching the photo album, he mounted and rode slowly toward town.

It was getting dark, and he hoped he could catch Molinari in his office. The small building was a trap, as he well knew, but if he worked it right, it would be a cage for the photographer. He didn't have much of a plan, but without real leverage over the man, Slocum was at a loss how else to proceed. He needed Molinari alive to show him where he had hidden the blackmail photographs, but getting that information was going to be difficult.

Slocum dismounted some distance down the street and stood in the gathering shadows, watching the photographic studio for any sign that Molinari had laid a trap for him. The door stood open to admit the growing evening breeze and dispel some of the heat from within the building. If Molinari had been taking pictures inside, the room would be hotter than Hades. Every flash added fumes to the air and more than a little heat. After ten minutes, all Slocum saw was Molinari moving around inside.

There wasn't any sign of his two henchmen. They might

have hightailed it after the shoot-out when he freed Sara Beth, but he couldn't count on it. Not with his own life on the line. Slocum knew failure now meant disgrace for at least three women.

Slocum drew his six-shooter and held it at his side. In his left hand he held Emily's photo album in front of him to distract the photographer. He kicked the door open all the way so that it slammed with a loud bang against the wall. Molinari jumped a foot, his eyes wide with shock at the sudden noise.

"I've got this, Molinari," Slocum said. "Where're the rest?"

"Slocum. I thought you were dead."

"Is that what your gunmen told you?"

"They said they'd run into trouble and had lost a very expensive camera. I hadn't realized the trouble was you, and that they lied about ambushing you."

"They've tried enough times."

Molinari recovered some of his aplomb. He smoothed wrinkles from his coat.

"Reach for a hideout gun, and I'll cut you down where you stand."

"No, you won't. You know what I'll do. If I'm dead, all the pictures will be released." Molinari pointed to the book Slocum still held in front of him. "Did you like my dirty dozen?"

"What?"

"That's what I call them. I keep twelve of the most, shall we say, interesting, pictures of each subject. There is something about a dozen that seems so right to me. I can show off the subject from every angle—so anyone looking at the album would fully realize the model's beauty."

"One's missing," Slocum said. "You sent that to Emily Dawson and that's why she killed herself."

Molinari shrugged.

"Probably so. She was so young when those were taken. Hardly sixteen would be my guess. She worked at one of the highest-class brothels in Kansas City, but she thought she was too good for that."

"You lost track of her when she married Henry Dawson."

"I didn't even know she'd married, much less a preacher man." Molinari moved around and perched on the edge of his desk, one leg swinging. Slocum knew better than to be distracted by such motion when dealing with a snake like Molinari. He watched the photographer's eyes for any hint of trouble to come. It bothered him that Molinari was relaxing now. He thought he had the upper hand.

Worse, Slocum *knew* he did.

"Keeping such mementos pays off. As you know. How did you figure out I was blackmailing Philomena Bray?"

"That doesn't matter. I want all your photographs."

"Or what?"

"I'll pay for them."

"You're broke," Molinari said. "But you might have money," he said, looking thoughtful. "From Severigne? No, not just from her. From Clabber as well as Severigne. He has such a lech for her, but it does no good. He had his balls blown off in the war, you know. His affection for her has its limits. She is such a vibrant woman. She needs more than he could ever offer."

"Where I get the money's no concern of yours."

"Might you have collected some from Martin Bray? No, I think not. His wife has bled dry his bank. If she had told him about how all that cash flowed from his vault to my pocket, he would disown her."

"Might be he wants to keep the photographs a secret."

"She does. He would be outraged. No, your money—if it even exists—must come from Clabber and Severigne. Why?"

"Severigne wants Missy to marry the rancher."

"Ah, the light begins to dawn. She wants to elbow me aside and take over the blackmail. You have seen the photograph, haven't you, Slocum? No, you haven't. Let me show you."

Slocum tried to hold down his anticipation. He had no

idea what pose Missy could have been in to ever drive away Hans Lehrer. When Molinari pulled it from his desk drawer, Slocum knew.

"The two of them in this picture. Both such lovely women, don't you agree? How would Missy's prospective hubby receive her if this picture of such amorous Sapphic activity was shown him? Not well."

"How'd you happen to take that?"

"Actually, Missy suggested it when I was working in Fort Smith. She enjoys women as much as men. More so, is my thought. But Lehrer could never bear such disgraceful behavior. Such *unnatural* behavior." Molinari laughed, and Slocum almost pulled the trigger.

"What about Anna?"

Molinari's laughter died and anger replaced it. He balled his fists.

"She was a stupid bitch. She thought she would defy me."

"So you killed her?"

"She killed herself with drugs. I only helped her along. Rather, my stupid assistant did. She—"

"She knew something about you and had to be killed."

"My idiot assistants should have killed you a long time ago."

"That," Slocum said, "would mean you couldn't sell all your photographs for a very large sum."

"Ten thousand dollars. I'll sell them for ten thousand."

"Five," Slocum said reflexively. He knew if he didn't dicker, Molinari would know he was bluffing. The bartering went on for what seemed a lifetime to Slocum until Molinari finally agreed on a sum.

"Eight thousand is a fair price for my dirty dozen. Or should I say, dirty dozens, since each album holds that many revealing poses."

"Anna's, too."

Molinari's anger flared again, then he settled down. From the glint in his eye, Slocum knew he was going to lie.

"Very well. Anna's will be included. But only Missy, Philomena, and Catherine's photos."

"Burn this." Slocum tossed Molinari Emily's album. "You don't need it anymore."

"As a show of good faith," Molinari said. "Very well." He went to the stove at the end of the room and built a small fire that turned the room into an oven. One photo at a time went into the fire until all were gone. "The book, too? Oh, yes, why not?" The photographer added the album to the dancing flames turned to greens and blues by the photographs.

"Where are the photographs you're selling?"

"Where's the money?"

Again they negotiated. Molinari finally relented and reluctantly said, "Very well. I will show you my precious dirty dozens but no more than a look until I have the money. And you have to put that hogleg into its holster and slip the thong over the hammer so you can't throw down on me. I suspect you're quite a gunslick, Slocum. Am I right?"

Slocum holstered his pistol and knew he was risking his life. Molinari would never agree to simply show him the photos without having at least some of the money in sight.

"I'm not like your partners," Slocum said.

"Ah, well, they had a checkered career before coming to me. They were both road agents until I showed them ways of making money that didn't require using a gun."

"I just got to town when they tried to kill me."

"Sometimes wild animals that have been tamed revert to their feral ways," Molinari said, grinning. "Can you blame them? You were far too interested in Anna's death."

Slocum knew what they had done to Sara Beth and probably others, all at Molinari's orders. He could blame them.

"Let's get on with it. Where are your files?"

"Not here, as you undoubtedly know. It was you who searched the place and shot it out with one of my assistants, wasn't it? I thought so." Molinari looked shrewdly at Slocum. "The gunfight destroyed valuable chemicals, and replacing them is going to be both time-consuming and costly."

"You'll have the money to buy all the damned chemicals you want," Slocum said.

"Ah, a flare of impatience. That surprises me. I had you pegged as a man of infinite patience. I see you like the mountain lion, lying on a tree limb above a game trail, choosing carefully which of the animals passing below to have for dinner. Not the first or even the second. They might be too scrawny. No, you'll wait for the one that suits you most perfectly, then you'll pounce."

"Enough," Slocum said. "The photographs." He reached for his pistol, but Molinari held up his hand.

"All right. You know I don't have them here. No loose floorboards. You would have checked. The plates are difficult to store but the photographs, even in albums, are not any more problem than putting a book or two on a shelf."

Slocum swept the room looking for a shelf holding books. He would have noticed before and this cursory examination revealed nothing.

"Not here. I have a secure spot outside town where I stored everything after your prior trespass."

"Close enough so we can walk?"

"You really don't trust me, do you? Yes, but it is a hike uphill. In fact, the storage place is quite close to the Bray house. I find that something of an irony."

Slocum remained silent. He was getting fed up with Molinari. When the photographer reached into his pocket and looked at his watch, Slocum knew he was walking into a trap but had no choice. Molinari would never have agreed to show the entire set of photographs without a stack of money close at hand. That glance meant the trap was already set, his two gunmen in place to cut Slocum down where the shots wouldn't be heard.

"Let's be off. The sooner you are convinced I have what I claim, the sooner you will give me your money," Molinari said.

As they left, Slocum tried to move the leather keeper off his Colt, but Molinari kept too close an eye on him to be able to do it without being seen. Slocum walked along, alert for a trap, but the shadows held only phantoms. After ten minutes of hiking, Slocum knew the ambush would be at the spot where Molinari claimed the blackmail photographs were hidden.

Whether they were there or not didn't matter. Slocum wanted the trio of blackmailing, kidnapping thieves all together so he could deal with them. He was tired of chasing them down, but he had to keep Molinari alive, at least for a while. Even if the photographer didn't come right out and tell him where the photographs were hidden, he could get clues from the way the man acted. Molinari was the kind who liked to boast. He'd hint and dance around the actual hiding place, thinking he was playing a game and was smarter than Slocum.

He might be smarter, but he wasn't more determined.

"Up ahead, up there!"

Molinari pointed at a woodpile a few yards distant. Both men jumped when someone noisily ran through the brush to their right side. Molinari turned around, stared at the woodpile, and yelled.

"Kill him now, you fools. You're letting him get away!"

Slocum slid off the leather loop and had his six-shooter out and firing when the first of Molinari's henchmen showed himself. Slocum hit him twice in the middle of the chest. It didn't kill him but put him out of action. The second gunman opened fire from the far side of the woodpile, shooting over it. The foot-long tongues of orange flame betrayed his position. Slocum focused his fire on the spot where a man would look down a rifle barrel. His fourth shot—the last in his six-gun—hit flesh. He heard a grunt and then there wasn't another sound.

"You fools. You fired too fast. He might have hit the plates." Molinari had dropped to his knees and threw cut wood back like a gopher digging a hole. "Where are they? You—"

Slocum walked toward Molinari, reloading as he came.

The photographer let out a yelp, clutched a large, heavy box to his chest, and bolted like a frightened deer. Slocum finished reloading, lifted his Colt, and emptied the cylinder at Molinari's fleeing figure. Then the photographer was swallowed by the dark of the forest. Slocum strained to hear footsteps but there was none. The gunfire had frightened the nocturnal animals and even the wind had ceased, as if it, too, were listening.

He went to the woodpile and saw where Molinari had stashed the box. Slocum frowned as he looked at the cavity formed by carefully stacking the wood. He dropped down to examine a space about the length of his forearm, from the elbow to the tip of his trigger finger. Peering closer, he saw two separate impressions in the damp earth.

One was the size of the case Molinari used for the photographic plates. From the way he had stumbled and staggered as he ran off, whatever he carried had been heavy.

The other indentation in the soft ground was shallow, hardly a quarter inch. Slocum pressed his finger down gently until he applied enough pressure to make a similarly deep dent. The size and weight were enough for the strongbox. But Molinari had carted off only one box. A heavy one.

The strongbox might have been weighty enough to make him struggle, but Slocum had heard Molinari cry out that he couldn't find something.

If he had the plates, where were the photographs?

Slocum suspected they had been spirited away by the shadowy figure that had ruined Molinari's ambush.

He reloaded, tucked away his pistol, and went to fetch the photographs. Molinari and the plates could wait. For a while.

20

Slocum sat in the dark, listening to the wind gently rustle the leaves. In the distance a coyote howled but nearer, perhaps at the foot of the tree, he heard small animals moving. A fox or a rabbit scurried about, hunting for food or being hunted and trying to avoid being another's food. He leaned back against the rough bark and closed his eyes. He felt tired but kept every sense alert.

He smelled the newcomer before he heard him. Peppermint. Peppermint candy. There came a twig snapping below him, then scraping sounds, and then the limb next to his sagged with weight.

"Hello, Edgar," he said softly. The boy jumped so hard he almost lost his balance.

"Didn't expect you to be here. Didn't expect anyone to be up here in my tree."

"You can look down on the world from here. Hide things, too," Slocum said. "But your usual hidey-hole is empty."

"You got the album," Edgar said. From his defensive tone Slocum knew there was more.

"I could have shot you earlier tonight."

"I don't know what you mean."

"Yes, you do. You were at the woodpile near the Bray house when the photographer and I were walking up the hill. Did we flush you?"

"Scared the hell outta me." Edgar clapped his hand over his mouth. "Pa don't want me talkin' like that. I'm sorry."

"I won't say a word if you tell me where you hid the photographer's box of pictures."

"Don't know what you mean."

"It's a strongbox, with a lock on it, but a clever boy like you could open it. Maybe take a rock to the hasp or pry open the lock. There were a hundred pictures inside."

"There were not!" Edgar flared. "There was only—"

"Twelve? There were only twelve albums?"

"Eleven," he said reluctantly, knowing he had been caught in the lie. "Reckon the one you took away from me might make twelve."

"I want them."

"Those are real purty women in those pictures, but I don't understand what's going on in some of them."

"I want the albums—all of them. Now." Slocum's voice was level and cold. He was tired of playing games with the boy. "You said you'd stop peeking through windows."

"I did. I ain't done that since. Not once. But I saw Mr. Molinari cartin' the two boxes up toward the Bray's house, so I followed him this afternoon. I thought he was actin' real funny, the way he hid those boxes and all. You know I couldn't look through his windows. They're all blacked out."

"You followed him and saw him hiding the boxes?"

"I wasn't gonna keep it. I just wanted to look. One box was too big and heavy for me to take, but the iron box wasn't so big."

"Where is it?"

"I won't steal again either. Honest."

Slocum waited. Edgar finally broke down and said, "In my special hiding place. I'll show you."

The boy climbed down the tree with surprising speed.

Slocum was slower to follow, and by the time his boots touched ground, Edgar was heading off at a dead run. Slocum followed at a brisk walk. There wasn't any place for the boy to hide in Clabber Crossing. All it would take was to ask and everyone would know where he was. Slocum didn't think the boy was the kind to run away, but considering what he'd been up to, he might.

Considering how he had lost his ma and how he said his pa shunned him when he was bad, ignoring him and making him feel all alone, he might think running away was the answer.

Slocum walked faster and saw the boy at the corner of the church. He ducked behind it. When Slocum got around to the rear, the boy was on his knees prying loose a rock in the foundation. At the bottom of the huge hole there was the strongbox with Molinari's blackmail photographs in it. How Edgar had removed the lock wasn't anything that mattered to Slocum. As he had said, the boy was clever.

Dragging it out, Slocum counted the albums. He had no reason to look through them, but he knew the boy already had.

"You see anyone you recognized in these pictures?"

"A couple of them Cyprians that work out at the place where you do."

"Missy and Catherine?"

"Those are the ones. I recognized them right off since they don't wear much around the cathouse."

"And you saw them through the window." Slocum nodded. The boy could identify them because they matched their photographs. But he hadn't recognized his mother. At least Slocum hoped the boy hadn't. He was a liar but there was still time to get him back on the straight and narrow.

"Yeah. They wore different frilly things, but they was the same. All except the one. Missy. Why was she with another woman in—"

"Never mind," Slocum said sharply. He picked up the box. "Reputations can be ruined. You know what that means?"

"What everyone thinks about you."

"You never saw these photographs. You never looked through windows at the ladies."

"I never stole anything," the boy said, looking at Slocum.

"You never stole anything. You're starting over. A clean slate. That's you now. Bust a window with your slingshot or tip over an outhouse, but you'll never spy on anyone again, especially women."

"Yes, sir."

Slocum swung the box up to his shoulder. It was heavy but nowhere near as heavy as the case containing the photographic plates. Molinari might not have some of the plates any longer. Destroy the pictures and the blackmail material would be eradicated. The plates he did have might be mostly those taken of the ladies for Severigne's catalog.

If so, Molinari was plum out of luck with any more blackmailing.

That meant he had to get rid of the plates and at whatever price he could get and then clear out. With his gunmen dead and Slocum on his trail, he couldn't run far enough.

"You ain't gonna tell my pa?"

"You can tell him what you like," Slocum said. "How much depends on how clear you want your conscience to be." He struck out down the hill, circled past the shack where Edgar's ma had shot herself, then cut across the field and reached Severigne's house in less than twenty minutes.

He wasn't surprised to see Molinari's buckboard out front. The photographer had probably come straight here after throwing together what he could from his office, intent on hitting the trail and getting the hell away from Clabber Crossing.

Softly, Slocum went in the back door and made his way down the narrow corridor to the parlor where he heard Molinari's strident voice telling Severigne what she had to do. He ought to have realized that wasn't the way to convince the fiery Frenchwoman of anything.

"A thousand dollars. For all of them. You can put your own books together, sell them to your customers. You'll make twice off a single client that way."

"You have done this thing, selling the pictures?"

"During the war. The soldiers paid incredible amounts of money for a single photo. Sometimes an entire company would pool their money. I got a hundred dollars a photograph for the best. And all these? These are even better."

"I do not know how to turn the glass plate into a paper photograph."

"Over in Laramie is a photographer who'll help with that. I . . . I have to go."

"Stay for a cup of tea," Slocum said, coming into the room. Molinari's eyes went wide in surprise, then he pulled back his coat. He wore a shoulder rig with a small six-shooter dangling in it. Slocum drew and fired three times before Molinari yanked it free.

"You shot him," Severigne accused.

"Looks like."

"Don't just stand there. Get him off the table. That is oak. Do you know what blood stains do to oak? Impossible to get out!"

By now Alice, Missy, April, and two others had rushed down to see what was happening.

"There're the photographs you wanted," Slocum said to Severigne. He heaved Molinari's lifeless body over his shoulder and went out the front. Alice opened the door for him. He dumped the corpse in the back of the buckboard, rummaged around, and found Molinari's bags and took them back into the house, intending to see if he might have loose copies of the pictures.

"These are . . . remarkable," Severigne said. Slocum saw she had stopped at Missy's. She looked up. Missy had turned white as a ghost. Silently, Severigne held out the album.

"When's the wedding?" Slocum asked.

"I couldn't, not after . . ."

"Missy," Slocum said louder. "When's your wedding?"

The woman clutched the book to her breasts and began crying.

"Soon," Alice said, answering for her. "As soon as she can go to Hans and explain she just had cold feet."

"I do not. My feet are always warm. Ask Hans," Missy said. Then she giggled. The giggle turned into hysterical laughter as Alice led her from the room. The other girls followed them, chattering about the wedding and arguing over who got to be maid of honor.

"What do you do with the rest?"

"Burn them, all except Philomena's," Slocum said. "Those go back to her so she'll know she doesn't have anything to fret over."

Severigne nodded. She hiked one of Molinari's carpetbags to the table and began going through it. She stepped back, her eyes fixed on the contents, and her jaw dropped. She looked up at Slocum.

"Do you know what this is?"

Slocum tipped the bag on its side and spilled out more greenbacks than he could remember seeing in his life.

"He could have run a long way with this much."

"He didn't care about the money," Slocum said. "He lusted after the power the photographs gave him. The money was only a way of keeping track of how much influence he had over helpless women trying to better themselves."

"This is all stolen money," Severigne said. "There is no way to tell whose it is." She obviously fought a battle with herself, then said, "It is yours. You have earned it."

"There're thousands of dollars there," Slocum said.

"You will get rid of the body so no one ever finds it?"

"The wagon and the photographic equipment inside will be harder to get rid of, but I think I know how."

Severigne made shooing motions.

"I will destroy these. Such lovely photographs, but I will burn them all." Severigne let out a gusty sigh. "It is no good having a conscience, not in this business." She smiled broadly. "But sometimes it makes you feel good." She leaned forward, her weight on the stack of albums.

Slocum took the carpetbag stuffed with scrip and went outside to the buckboard. After making sure everything was secure in the back, he got his horse, tied it to the back of the wagon, and began driving.

Two days later an hour after dinnertime he rode back into town carrying the carpetbag across the front of his saddle. He rode to the foot of the hill where the Bray house stood, considered what he was going to do—then he did it.

Slocum trooped up to the house and peered in through a window, feeling like Edgar Dawson. Philomena Bray sat in a chair doing needlepoint. She looked up and started to cry out but Slocum held up the album, showing just one page. She stuck herself with the needle and didn't even notice the tiny drop of blood that stained her work. Slocum pointed to the rear of the house. The woman came out on the back porch, pale and distraught.

"Where did you get that?" Philomena was shaking like a leaf in a high wind. "What are you going to do with it?"

Slocum handed it to her.

"It's yours to do with as you see fit. It's a sultry night but you might want to start a fire," he said, looking past her at the fancy iron stove.

"He . . . he doesn't have any more?"

"You won't see him or his pictures again," Slocum said. The deep ravine out on the lonesome prairie where he had buried both body and buckboard might wash out but that wouldn't be until spring runoffs in nine months. By then Molinari would be little more than a memory to the people of Clabber Crossing.

Slocum had taken special care smashing every one of the photographic plates before scattering the pieces far and wide across the prairie.

"Thank you," Philomena said, crushing him with a hug. He pushed her away and handed her the carpetbag.

"What's this?" She looked inside and began to wobble on her feet. He caught her before she fainted dead away.

"I don't know how much you paid him, but this is likely most of it," Slocum said. "However you took it from your husband, you can put it back the same way."

"Why are you doing this?"

"I like to see things all neat and tidy."

"How do I ever repay you?"

"Keep that son of yours out of fights he can't win. He's got an attitude that'll see him up on Primrose Hill before long if he doesn't change."

Slocum felt as if the morals of Clabber Crossing's younger citizens were his responsibility—and he had discharged his duties the best he could when it came to Randall Bray and Edgar Dawson.

"Philly, where are you?"

"That's Martin. I had better see what he wants."

Slocum tipped his hat, stepped back, and disappeared into the night.

Leading his tired horse, he walked back down to Main Street, where Clyde Clabber waved to him.

"Come on over, Slocum. You been away for a couple days?"

"Call it completing my tour of duty with Severigne," Slocum said.

"She's a mighty fine woman, that Severigne," Clabber said. "Mighty fine."

Slocum took out a sheaf of bills. He had kept some of Molinari's ill-gotten money as his due.

"You up for a poker game?"

"Now, now, Slocum, you can't be serious. Remember what I did to you last time. You want me to do it again? You'll be here through next year's rodeo, if you have a hand like you had before—and I still have my four little ladies."

"Luck's riding on my shoulder 'bout now," Slocum said.

And it was. He won enough that night to pay for a month of breakfasts at Sara Beth's, as if she ever let him pay.